LITTLE
MERMAID

THE OFFICIAL MOVIE
NOVELISATION

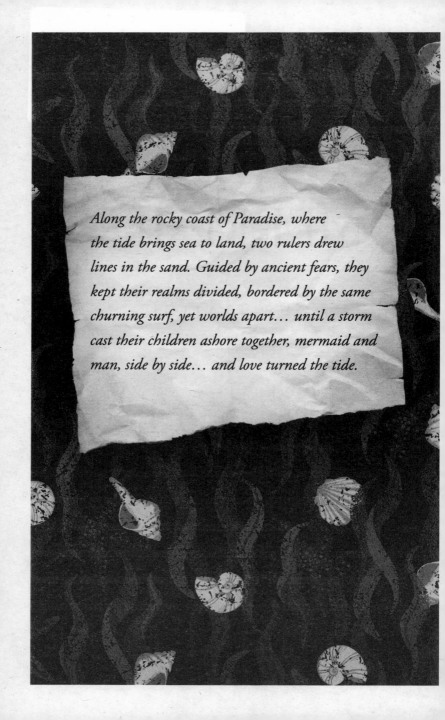

Along the rocky coast of Paradise, where
the tide brings sea to land, two rulers drew
lines in the sand. Guided by ancient fears, they
kept their realms divided, bordered by the same
churning surf, yet worlds apart… until a storm
cast their children ashore together, mermaid and
man, side by side… and love turned the tide.

Prologue

The sea is filled with a myriad of wild, dangerous beasts, but none more dangerous than the ruthless merfolk. At least, that's the rumour. As the sailors aboard a trade ship catch sight of a shadowy form just below the ocean's surface, one thought races through all their minds: *Could this be a mermaid?*

There's a flurry of activity on the deck, with their excitement growing at the thought of seizing a creature no one's ever captured before. Mulligan, a crewman made rough from years at sea, leads the other sailors forwards.

"More harpoons!" he yells. "Ready the nets, men!" Several sailors crowd the ship's railing, hoping to catch a glimpse of the mermaid. A barbed spear is launched down through the water. It narrowly misses the creature.

Meanwhile, Eric stands high up on the rigging, looking far more like an average sailor than a prince. He has always felt more at home on the sea than on land. Out here he is free from the judgement and constraints of royal life. He's lost in his own world as he furls the sails to prepare for rough weather.

The commotion below grows louder. "I say kill her before she comes aboard!" cries Hawkins, an old deckhand. The others chant in agreement as they prepare their weapons and nets. Who knows what a live mermaid could do!

Eric pauses as Hawkins' comment, followed by the splash of a weapon hitting water, catches his ear. He glances down just as another harpoon is thrown. It misses its target again.

"Ahh, she's a fast one," Mulligan says. He gestures towards the harpoons. "Give me another!"

Horrified, Eric swings down from the rigging and pushes his way through the crowd. "Move! Get back! What are you doing?" Eric grabs Mulligan's arm an instant before the sailor throws another weapon.

"It's a mermaid, sir!" Mulligan says, his voice full of fervour.

Seriously? Eric inwardly groans. "A mermaid? Use your eyes!"

The prince gestures to the water as the sea creature majestically breaches the surface. It's a dolphin. It does a little spin in the water before swimming away. The sailors all fall silent.

"What were you thinking?" Eric folds his arms as he looks at the crowd with disappointment.

It is clear Mulligan isn't sure whether to be brazen or sheepish. "Well, these are dangerous waters."

"And this is a dangerous time," Hawkins adds. "Tonight is the Coral Moon." He pushes his way closer to Eric's side as the prince starts reeling in the ropes attached to the harpoons. Hawkins lowers his voice before continuing. "They say this is when the sea king calls his mermaid daughters together to lure men to their deaths."

"Is that what they say?" Eric frowns. He remembers hearing tales from his mother about the cruel, perilous merfolk. Even when he was a child, that idea had seemed so far-fetched to him.

"Aye!" Hawkins cries, his voice rising once more. "With siren songs so sweet and pure that not even the strongest can resist their spell."

"It's just an old lore," Eric says. *And a silly one at that,* he thinks. He grabs on to the railing as a gust of wind causes the boat to lurch. "All right, back to work!"

The men start to disperse, but Hawkins is still vexed. He follows Eric across the ship, convinced that any unsteady movement is proof enough of a nefarious sea king – not to mention the mermaids. The next rock of the ship sends Hawkins stumbling.

"You see there?" Hawkins calls to Eric as he attempts to catch his balance.

"Crosswind gust kicked up the chop, that's all." Eric pauses to help a crew member tie some loose netting.

Hawkins scoffs. "The sea king would pull us under himself if he could."

Eric notices a spritsail that has caught the wind and got tangled on the bowsprit. He starts to make his way towards it, but Hawkins catches his arm.

"And mermaids? Heartless creatures. They say they have no tears." Hawkins points to his own eye for emphasis.

"Well," Eric says, managing to shake himself from Hawkins' grasp, "I suppose they must feel everything that much more deeply."

With that, he strides away, leaving Hawkins to mutter under his breath. In truth, Eric doesn't know whether he believes in mermaids or any of the many creatures of lore. If they do exist, he can't imagine them to be the horrible beings his men describe. For all his mother's descriptions of cruel and heartless creatures, her stories also mentioned traditions and celebrations and families. If anything, mermaids are probably misunderstood. At any rate, this isn't the time to be wasting resources shooting at dolphins. They're starting to hit rough waters and need to be prepared. Eric shinnies onto the ship's narrow bowsprit to free the spritsail rope. He nearly loses his balance when the ship lurches again, but he manages to catch himself.

"Eric! What are you doing out there? Get back here at once!"

Looking down, Eric grins when he sees Sir Grimsby, the prime minister and his mentor. He looks a little green, but the expression of combined worry and exasperation on his face is one the young prince is all too familiar with.

"You ought to stop worrying so much about me, Grimsby," Eric calls to him.

Grimsby raises an eyebrow at the prince's light tone. "Call me selfish, but I do not want to tell the queen that her son fell overboard on my watch – and on his birthday, of all days."

Something in the distance catches Eric's eye before he can respond. A thrill goes through him. "Hey! Looks like there's a ship out there headed towards the mainland. We could follow them to port, see what they've brought to trade." The prince jumps back onto the deck and makes his way towards Grimsby. He takes a spyglass from Grimsby and raises it.

"Our ship is loaded to the gills as it is!" Grimsby argues. "We've risked our necks out here for seven weeks already. We're going home – tonight!"

But Eric isn't focused on Grimsby's words. He's already envisioning all the wonderful things out there to learn and explore. An entire world. Grimsby may be done after seven weeks, but Eric could never have enough time out on the sea. He leans over the railing for a better look. Grimsby, unimpressed, snatches the spyglass from his hand.

"Eric, please! Pay attention," he chides him. "I need you to be more careful— *Ohhh!*" The ship is rocked again by a heavy wave. Grimsby loses his balance, and the spyglass slips from his grip and falls overboard.

It sinks beneath the surface and winks out of sight. Eric sighs. He supposes it'll be something for the mermaids to enjoy now.

Chapter One

Nothing is quite as magnificent as the world under the sea. On first glance, there is a captivating calm that permeates the boundless expanse. Colourful plants sway gently, dancing among the tall rock formations that tower from the sandy seafloor. And hidden far from human eyes, a majestic palace of coral is centred perfectly within a luscious garden of blues and pinks.

Of course, the real beauty of the sea is the way it teems with life. From his throne, King Triton can see bales of sea turtles floating by while dolphins playfully dance around each other, chittering away. Schools of fish dart through the water, trying to keep up with each other. And all around him are the sounds of music and happy chatter as the palace merfolk make hasty preparations.

Tonight the Coral Moon celebrations begin.

It is the sea king's favourite time of year. It's when merfolk near and far gather to celebrate the moon's blessing of good luck and abundance. Most important, it's one of the few opportunities for Triton to see all his daughters gathered together. There is always work to be done but also much joy to be had so long as everything remains on track.

Triton puts a large conch shell to his lips and blows. The trumpeting sound blares throughout the waters. The sea king's daughters know what this means. It doesn't take long for the princesses to make their way into their father's throne room. King Triton's stature suggests great might and power, but there is a lightness within him as he looks around. His family is together, safe, ready to start a new year. Triton takes a seat on the natural carved throne in the centre of the room. His daughters settle on the coral ledges all around him.

"My daughters of the Seven Seas," he begins, beaming with pride, "it fills my heart to have you all here." He says to each of them in turn, "Tamika, Perla – it's so good to see you. Caspia, Indira – I welcome news from all your waters. Mala, Karina…" A noticeable gap catches his attention, and he pauses. "Where's Ariel?"

There is an uncomfortable pause as his daughters stare helplessly at each other. None of them have ever been too successful at keeping an eye on their youngest sister.

Triton starts to massage his temples, his frustration only increasing at the silence. All he wanted was a smooth start to this important celebration with *all seven* of his daughters. Was that too much to ask?

Most of the time, ruling the Seven Seas seems easy compared to keeping track of Ariel. She has never been one to stay still for long. She has too much of an adventurous spirit. It's frightening how much she reminds him of her mother. A lump rises in his throat at the thought. He shakes his head to clear it and refocuses on the problem at hand.

He notices a sudden movement out of the corner of his eye. He sees Sebastian, his right-hand crab, attempting to scutter quietly away. Frowning, Triton reaches out and pins Sebastian under his finger.

"Sebastian!" The crab shakes as Triton's nostrils flare angrily. "You were supposed to see to it that Ariel was here!"

"Oh, I tried, Your Majesty, but that child, she is impossible! I reminded her about the gathering just this morning. What else can one crustacean do?"

"You can go find her! Yes?" Triton releases his grip on the crab.

"Yes, Your Majesty! Right away!" Sebastian scurries away as fast as his little legs will allow.

Triton watches him go before pinching the bridge of his nose. It is so like his youngest child to miss an important event because she is off exploring the seas or some such nonsense. Why can't she be less... curious? No, that's not what he wants. As much as her behaviour frustrates him, there's a calming familiarity to even Ariel's most exasperating quirks. The thought slowly melts away Triton's anger, leaving the sea king lost in an old memory.

Meanwhile, Sebastian grumbles to himself as he makes his way out of the throne room. "How hard can it be to find a mermaid?" And wasn't that always the question with Ariel? If he's lucky, he'll have to search only *one* ocean. The crab sighs deeply. "Where are you, child?"

* * *

Ariel swims leisurely through the water, keeping her eyes open for any interesting treasures hiding themselves among the rocks and corals. She woke up this morning with the urge to explore burning in her belly. It's been a few days since she's found anything new to add to her collection. She's a bit further out from the palace than she knows she's supposed to be, but the best objects can be discovered only out where the human shipwrecks settled.

The glint of something in a crevice among the rocks catches Ariel's eye. She reaches for the shiny unfamiliar treasure.

"Haven't seen one of these before," she mumbles to herself. It has a long cylindrical shape, with one side larger than the other. Ariel's fascinated smile spreads from ear to ear as she lifts the large end to her face and squints through it. She sees her friend Flounder on the other side. The timid young fish, looking impossibly small, swims towards her.

"We aren't supposed to be this far from the palace, Ariel," Flounder says.

She is surprised at how near his voice sounds. She's even more surprised when she lowers the object and sees that Flounder is much closer than he appeared. "Oh!"

"Let's go back," Flounder begs.

But the strange device has captured Ariel's attention.

How does it work? She raises and lowers it, watching things around her shift from big to small. Humans create such interesting objects. How could anyone not be intrigued?

"Come on, Ariel. Please!"

She grins at her friend's typical behaviour. He looks like he's fighting the urge to see if he can wrap his little fins around her arm and drag her away. "Oh, Flounder. Stop being such a guppy."

"I'm not a guppy." He is unable to keep the pout from his voice.

Ariel playfully raises an eyebrow but doesn't contradict him. She swims over a rise and raises the object, looking through the small end this time. A thrill runs through her as she sees that things in the distance appear much closer. Now *this* is useful.

"I think we've gone far enough," Flounder continues. But Ariel catches a glimpse of a group of jagged rocks, littered with the wrecked hulls and rotting timber of sunken ships.

"Wait, what is that?" She has explored this shipwreck graveyard countless times, much to her father's consternation, but she's certain she hasn't seen this wreck before. Ariel's stomach flutters. A new wreck means new things to explore. "Come on!" she says to Flounder as she lowers the object. It collapses in on itself, and she tucks it into the treasure bag she keeps strapped across her shoulder. Delighted, she races off.

Flounder jumps, panicked. He watches Ariel head towards the mass of giant creaking ship remains. Even from this far away he can feel the large debris loom over them. He doesn't want to go anywhere near it, but he wants to be left behind even less. "Ariel, wait for me! You know I can't swim that fast."

The new shipwreck has probably carried dozens, maybe even hundreds, of humans in its time. The ship itself appears mostly intact, though it's surrounded by broken glass and sharp splinters of wooden beams. There's a gaping hole in the centre of the ship's hull – a perfect invitation! Ariel peers inside. Debris is strewn around, but there are many strange treasures wanting to catch her eye. "Look at all that!" Awe fills her voice. "They must have used this ship for battles or something."

Flounder finally catches up to her, wheezing. "Yeah, great. Now let's get out of here."

"Getting cold fins?" Ariel grins, biting back a laugh, before swimming into the ship.

"Who, me? No way."

"Good. Then you can stay out here and watch for sharks." She tosses him a wink before swimming out of view.

"*What?* Ariel – wait!" Flounder cries as he swims into the ship. He looks around apprehensively as a shadow passes over the ship's hull.

Ariel ignores Flounder's squeals of protest as she moves through the gangway. She notices a door halfway off its hinges, creating the perfect entrance. Ariel pushes it aside just as Flounder catches up to her again. His eyes dart around nervously.

"Do you really think there might be sharks around here?"

"Oh, Flounder." Ariel chuckles. Her friend can be a scaredy-fish sometimes, but it rarely keeps him from joining her adventures. That makes her glad. She loves getting to discover new things with him.

Many of the human objects inside are in pieces across the floor. Ariel begins sorting through them, hoping to find something left intact to add to her collection.

Ariel gasps and pulls a small shiny object from a pile of scrap on a table. "Look at this!" She holds it up so Flounder can see. The tiny object is silvery, with three sharp points, and barely bigger than her hand. "It's the smallest trident I've ever seen!"

"Whoa," Flounder marvels, taking a closer look. He may be a nervous fish, but he is just as amazed by these human treasures as Ariel.

She playfully jabs the tiny trident towards her friend. "I'm King Flounder," she says in a deep, kingly voice. "Lord of the Seven Seas!"

Flounder giggles. "I wonder why a human would need one that size."

"I bet Scuttle would know. She always does," Ariel says, dropping the tiny trident into her bag. She is distracted by the sight of a large sheet covering something. She tugs it away and comes face to face with her own image. Ariel has seen a mirror once before, but not one this large. Flounder gives a startled cry when he sees himself.

Ariel can't help laughing. "Will you relax? It's just your reflection. Calm down. Nothing is going to happen—"

But as she glances at the mirror again, a third figure appears, looming larger and larger in the mirror's reflection.

A shark.

Chapter
Two

Ariel spins around to find the shark nearly at the window behind Flounder.

"Flounder! Look out!"

He turns just as the shark crashes through the window. The creature bites widely. Ariel barely moves fast enough. The shark snaps at her tail, and as she swivels to avoid the attack, she drops her bag. A brief flutter of panic fills her chest at the thought of losing her treasure, but her focus is quickly stolen as the shark angrily bares its teeth at them. Ariel and Flounder race out of the room and down the gangway. They swim as fast as they can. Ariel's heart pounds. Getting eaten was definitely *not* part of her plans for today.

Ariel pauses once they reach the other end of the ship. An eerie silence settles over them, making her tense. She realises she doesn't hear the shark moving any more.

"Ariel…" Flounder whispers.

She hesitantly looks around. Is it gone?

Crash! The shark suddenly bursts through the hull behind them. It's so close Ariel can feel the heat of its breath on her tail. The shark's momentum sends it crashing to the floor, and Ariel and Flounder immediately take off. The shark doesn't stay down long, though. Its fin tears through the floor and rips up floorboards as it chases after them. They dive through another hole in the ship, but the shark smashes through the side wall, sending debris everywhere. Ariel swims faster. She and Flounder need to keep getting distance from the shark, and—

Ariel freezes when she realises she can't see Flounder any more. Her gaze darts around frantically. *Oh, Flounder, where are you?* She finally spots his hiding place – at the same time the shark does.

"Flounder!" she cries. She has to do something – now. Through a hole in the wall, she catches a glimpse of her reflection in the mirror they uncovered earlier. An idea sparks.

It's not unusual for one of Ariel's ideas to result from little planning and quick thinking. She does not hesitate. She pushes a loose barrel towards the shark. It looks up and trains its eyes on her. Its fierce teeth curve into an almost smile before it rockets towards her. Ariel swims through the hole, back into the first room she was in.

Moments later the shark bursts inside, heading straight forwards. Ariel can tell it's ready to devour her. Lucky for her, it doesn't notice that it is actually diving towards Ariel's reflection. The shark crashes through the mirror, its body getting stuck in the heavy round frame.

Ariel: one; shark: zero.

Flounder immediately swims towards the real Ariel.

For a moment they watch as the shark struggles in vain to escape. Ariel then glances down and sees her bag of treasures right where she dropped it. Relief floods through her. *Can't leave here without this,* she thinks. She grabs the bag and scoops Flounder inside before speeding out of the ship.

The shark may be trapped, but Ariel doesn't slow down until they make it to the edge of an ocean shelf near the water's surface. Beams of sunlight break through, brightening up the space in a way that makes it seem safer, more open. No sharks are hiding up here. Ariel releases Flounder from her bag and frowns as she notices his trembling.

"You okay?" she asks him. She can't help feeling a tiny bit guilty for almost getting her best friend eaten.

Flounder tries to put on a brave face and nods. "Sure. I mean, I've seen bigger sharks." He puffs up in a show of bravado. "Just, you know... you can't back down. You gotta show them who's in char— *Ahh!*" He darts for cover as a seabird suddenly dives through the water, racing past them.

Ariel shakes her head. Some things never change. "Come back, Flounder. It's just Scuttle."

They watch as their friend Scuttle, an eccentric seabird, grabs a minnow and surfaces. She dives back down to greet them and swims to the ledge.

"Ariel! Hey, kid, how're you doing? Don't mind me. I was just grabbing a snack."

Ariel holds up her bag for Scuttle to see. "Look! We found more treasure!"

"Yeah, we went into this sunken ship," Flounder adds. He makes a face and shudders. "It was really creepy."

"Human stuff!" Scuttle hops forwards, her beak curved into a smile. She's the only one whose level of excitement ever matches Ariel's when it comes to objects from above the surface. "All right, all right, lemme see!"

"Any idea what this is?" Ariel holds out the tiny trident to Scuttle.

Scuttle peers at it closely. In truth she has no idea what it is, but Scuttle's motto has always been *when in doubt, make it up*. "Wow, yes," she says, nodding sagely. "This is very, very unusual."

Ariel eagerly leans forwards. "What? What is it?" Dozens of ideas run through her mind. Is it a toy weapon for play battles? Is it used for decoration? Maybe it helps them open things?

Scuttle clears her throat and gives a confident nod. "This is… a dinglehopper!"

"A dinglehopper," Ariel says, her voice filled with wonder. *Scuttle knows so many amazing things.*

"Yeah," Scuttle continues. "Humans use these babies to style their hair. You just give it a little twirl. A little yank." Scuttle demonstrates, combing it through her feathers. "You might get some pieces with it, and you're left with an artistically pleasing conflagration of hair that humans go nuts for."

Delighted, Ariel uses the dinglehopper to twirl a lock of her hair. "I would love to see that."

"Can't," says Flounder, a bubble-bursting voice of reason.

"Flounder!" Ariel chides him.

"You know it's true."

Scuttle nods understandingly. "Your father still won't let you go to the surface, huh?"

"Nope. It's forbidden. He thinks all humans are barbarians." She doesn't understand why her father gets so stubborn when it comes to humans. Everything she has ever found from their shipwrecks makes them seem thoughtful and creative. There is probably so much they could learn from the humans if her father would just be open to it.

Sighing, Ariel pulls the dinglehopper from her hair and places it back in her bag.

"Oh, they're not so bad," Scuttle says before pausing thoughtfully. "Well, unless you're a coconut. They hate coconuts. I swear, they get a hold of one, they smash it to pieces just like that." Scuttle knocks her head on the ledge for emphasis. "It's weird."

Ariel reaches into her bag to take out another interesting object she managed to nab from before. It's a funny-looking instrument, about the size of her palm. It's long and skinny on one end and curves up into a large bowl shape. Ariel twirls it around in her hand before holding it out to Scuttle. "And what's this?"

Scuttle opens her mouth to give her own elaborate description when a voice from below causes them all to jump.

"ARIEL!"

Startled, Ariel drops the object. She looks down to see it clonk the head of Sebastian, her father's majordomo.

"Ari— *OWW!*"

Oops! Ariel covers her laugh with her hand. "Sorry about that!"

The disapproval on Sebastian's face is clear. "Ariel! What are you doing up there? Wasting your time with this know-nothing bird that can't tell swimming from flying?"

"Hey!" Scuttle squawks.

Sebastian ignores her. "And I suppose you've completely forgotten tonight's the Coral Moon?"

Ariel's eyes widen. She isn't sure how it could have slipped her mind. "Oh, no!"

"Oh, yes! The gathering of Triton's daughters, *minus one!*" Sebastian waves an accusatory claw at her.

"Oh, my father's going to kill me!" Ariel has been late to other gatherings, but never one as important as the Coral Moon celebration. Her father will be so angry. Worse, he might fix her with that disappointed stare that always makes her feel smaller than plankton. "Sorry, Scuttle, gotta go!"

Scuttle assures her it's fine before heading to the surface. Ariel quickly swims off, with Flounder and Sebastian close behind her. Not a single one of them has noticed that they were being watched.

* * *

Way deep in a dark corner of the sea, where the life and vibrancy of Triton's kingdom has not reached, Ursula waits. Her pet eels, Flotsam and Jetsam, follow Ariel as she races towards the palace. The sea witch sits back, observing it all in a large black pearl floating in the centre of her lair.

Ursula smiles bitterly to herself. "Yes, hurry home, Princess. We wouldn't want to be late for Daddy's gathering, now would we? Perhaps I'll join them – Oh, wait!" She pretends to look around for a non-existent invitation. "What a shame… It seems they forgot to invite Ursula *again*!"

She has a strong urge to hit something but settles for reaching with one of her squid-like tentacles into a cage and plucking out a live shrimp.

Ursula lets out an enraged shriek. "I should be the one throwing parties! Not waiting on my invitation." She stuffs the shrimp into her mouth and spits out the shell. She can barely taste a thing in her anger.

Look at me, Ursula thinks. *Wasting away to practically nothing. And for what?* For fifteen long years she has lived in exile, banished and driven to boredom in this dim little crevice.

Sometimes Ursula looks around herself and is overcome by a wave of sadness. It is very cold in this part of the sea. It is even lonelier. She has her eels, of course. Flotsam and Jetsam are her pride and joy. But Ursula was not meant to be such a solitary creature. When she was a young squid, everyone knew her as the life of the party. Some called her loud and dramatic, but no one could deny she was a master entertainer. Now here she is, muttering to herself.

"All while Daddy and his spoiled little mer-brats celebrate the Coral Moon!" Sadness quickly leaves to make room for fury. It's not fair!

Deep breaths, Ursula, she reminds herself. This is not the time for wallowing in self-pity. If there's one thing that's true about Ursula, it's that she has never been one to stay down for long. She has been accruing magic of her own for the last decade and a half.

If those mermaids want something to celebrate, Ursula will give it to them. She reaches for the nautilus shell around her neck and twists it between her fingers as she leans in towards her black pearl. She watches Ariel in its inky depths. "I may have finally found Daddy's weakness after all." Ariel's fascination with humans might be just the opening Ursula has been waiting for. A smile creeps onto her face as she begins to form a plan.

Chapter Three

ontrary to what he is sure his youngest child believes, Triton does not enjoy yelling at his daughters. When Sebastian appears in the throne room with a sheepish Ariel and Flounder trailing behind him, the sea king tries to calm the swell of anger that immediately rises within him. He is not successful. He watches Ariel glance around as if she's hoping her sisters will pop out from behind the coral and tell her that she's right on time. But no one else is here, because she is late. *Again.*

He holds up a hand as Ariel opens her mouth to speak. "Do you realise how irresponsible this is? Your sisters are only here for one phase of the Coral Moon. Can you imagine any one of them missing the gathering?"

Ariel glances down at her fins and shakes her head. "No. You're right. I'm sorry."

Flounder swims forwards. "It wasn't Ariel's fault," he interjects. "We were… we were exploring, and a shark chased us, and—"

"A shark!" Triton exclaims. There aren't any sharks close to this palace, which can mean only one thing. "You went to the shipwrecks again. Those waters are dangerous!"

"You don't have to worry about me." Ariel crosses her arms defiantly.

It's almost funny how children never seem to understand the impossibility of such a thing. He reaches out and gives Ariel's arm what he hopes is a comforting squeeze. "I do worry, Ariel. This obsession with humans has to stop."

She sighs. "I just want to know more about them."

"You know all you need to know."

Ariel gives him an unimpressed look. "I barely know anything. You won't even let us go to the surface."

Not this again. Triton rubs his temples, his headache returning. "Why do you have to be so strong-minded? Just like your mother."

"I *am* her daughter."

The sea king hums in agreement. "Yes, foolish enough to be taken with the human world."

"If you would just try to understand—"

"I have tried," he says, his deliberate tone leaving no room for argument. At this point his patience is wearing thin. All he wants to do is protect his daughter, after not being able to protect…

He is tired of having this conversation. "I have tried to understand you long enough. But as long as you live in my ocean, you'll obey my rules." His voice rises, filled with a force that startles both him and Ariel. "Do you understand *that*?"

Ariel flinches. It's a tiny movement that greatly pains his heart. He hates seeing the hurt that is clear on her face. Still, he remains firm. He has to get through to her. They stare at each other for a beat longer before Ariel swims away without another word. Flounder hesitates for a moment before following her.

The sea king sighs. Sebastian scuttles up to him.

"Children – you give them an inch, they swim all over you."

Triton stares a moment longer at the spot his daughter left before he turns to Sebastian. "Was I too hard on her?" He used to hate it when his own father yelled. He wonders if he ever worried his parents half as much as Ariel worries him.

"Definitely not!" Sebastian assures him. "It's like I always say, children got to live by their parents' rules."

"You're absolutely right. My Ariel needs constant supervision."

Sebastian climbs up onto Triton's shoulder and bobs his head in agreement. "Constant."

"Someone to watch over her."

The crab continues nodding. "All the time, day and night."

"And you're just the crab to do it." Triton smiles.

"And I am just the crab to— Wait, what?" Sebastian backs away at the sea king's pointed look. "No, no, I serve *you*, Your Majesty, as your honoured majordomo."

"There is no better way you can serve me than to make sure my little one stays out of trouble." Triton imagines all the extra hours he'd have in his day if he didn't have to spend so much time worrying. It's a perfect plan.

Sebastian starts to protest again. "But I, ah—"

"Go! Go!" King Triton shoos the crab away. No better time to start than right away.

Resigned, Sebastian drops his head. "Yes, Your Majesty."

The crab marches from the throne room, mumbling

something about being an educated crustacean and not a babysitter for headstrong teenagers.

Triton knows the task leaves Sebastian less than enthused, but he really does need the help. He sighs and is hit with an overwhelming wave of longing. He misses his wife. How is he supposed to raise a child as elusive and stubborn as Ariel without her?

* * *

Ariel can barely see straight as she flees from the throne room. Her body moves of its own accord, leading her to the place that has become a refuge whenever she's feeling troubled: her hidden underwater grotto.

She discovered it by accident when she was in need of a hiding spot after a similar argument with her father. Since then, it has become her secret place, filled with the treasures she's collected over time. All around her are impressive brass fixtures, ivory carvings, books, paintings and bottles of every shape and size. Being surrounded by so many wonderful human things usually makes Ariel smile, but now she sits in the centre of them with her head lowered, feeling nothing but heavy hurt.

A concerned Flounder settles beside her. "Ariel, are you okay?"

"He doesn't even hear me!" Ariel sits up and lets out a frustrated sob. "I'm just not like him. I don't see things the way he does." He thinks she's the stubborn one, but she just wants him to *listen* to her. "I don't see how a world that makes such wonderful things could be so bad."

The creativity and ingenuity of humans amazes Ariel. The treasures she has discovered are beyond anything she could have dreamt up herself, and she's sure there are more out there.

Ariel picks up a small brass statue in the shape of an unfamiliar animal. Turning it gently between her fingers, she gazes at the object's reflective sheen. An incredibly sad girl frowns back at her.

She has always dreamt of seeing the world beyond their waters. It may be silly. She knows there's so much she has right here. She's the daughter of the powerful sea king, and she knows that her father loves her. It should be plenty, and yet...

As she moves through the grotto, her hands gently ghost over the different objects she has collected. Ariel closes her eyes and imagines herself running along the beaches with the sand under her feet. She wants to know how it feels to stand and let the sun beam down on her face. She wants to be away from the ocean's grip, to wander with a freedom she has never felt down here. She wants to feel connected to the great big world her mother always knew was out there.

Through the grotto's opening, Ariel can see the surface, where the moonlight tries to break through. She drifts upwards, reaching out her hand as if she can get close enough to touch it. There's a whole world up there, one she feels so close to and so far away from at the same time.

An unbearable yearning fills her heart. As she nears the grotto opening, a sudden burst of colourful light flashes across the night sky. What's happening up there?

Curiosity burns all the way to the tips of her fins. Her father may not understand, but she *needs* to break free. Ariel doesn't let herself think twice. She swims straight up through the grotto opening, towards the surface.

"Ariel, don't!" Flounder calls. But nothing can stop her now.

For the first time in her life, Ariel surfaces.

Chapter
Four

It's so colourful! That's Ariel's initial thought as she takes in life above the sea. The sky is alight with explosives that scatter rainbows of colour. She flinches as fire hits the water around her, but it doesn't lessen the grin that takes over her face. She has never seen anything like this before. This is the creativity she keeps trying to get her father to understand. The humans have made the night sky come alive!

The display mostly centres above a massive sailing ship, beautifully decorated with bright lanterns. The reddish Coral Moon hangs in the sky, illuminating everything.

Music and human voices drift over to Ariel. Intrigued, she swims towards them. She makes her way into a small lifeboat hanging from the ship's side. It doesn't let her view much more than a few legs and shoes dancing about, but she can hear people singing in celebration.

Ariel smiles. Their merriment is contagious. Making sure to stay out of view, she shifts to better observe the sights and conversations before her.

* * *

One thing is undoubtedly true: even in the middle of the ocean, sailors know how to throw a celebration. Tonight's raucous fete is to celebrate Prince Eric's birthday.

Men cheer as they blast fireworks into the sky. The sailors pass around food and drink as someone plays a fiddle. Eric sits in the centre of the deck, petting his fluffy sheepdog, Max, and grinning at the men around him as he joins them in bellowing an old shanty.

Eric finds himself getting into it, singing and dancing with his crew. He enjoys the rush that comes with such a carefree moment. For a little while he's able to forget that he's anything other than a regular sailor, unburdened by 'proper' responsibilities. But alas, Grimsby doesn't allow it to last.

"Thank you, gentlemen, thank you." Grimsby grabs Eric by the arm and guides him away from the others.

"Come on, Grimsby. What's wrong with me having a little fun? Everyone else is." Grimsby is a good man, but boy, can he be a killjoy sometimes.

"You, sire," Grimsby says, "are not everyone else. It's time you separated yourself from the rest of the crew—"

"But I'm one of them," Eric interjects.

"— and behave in a manner more becoming to a future king," Grimsby continues, straightening his gait as if simply talking about royal matters demands proper posture.

Eric bristles. He hates being reminded that he's a prince, that he's close to becoming a king. "You mean I should be more like my father was," he says, "cut off from the rest of the world." It's not the first time they've had this discussion. *It's time to get serious, Eric. You're not like everyone else.* Eric knows that Grimsby means well. He's just trying to prepare him for the inevitable future, but every time they discuss it, Eric feels more and more like he is being led to a prison sentence.

Grimsby places a hand on Eric's shoulder. Neither he nor Eric notices as Max wanders away, having spotted someone new peering through an opening in the ship's railing.

"You know what I mean, Eric," Grimsby says. He softens his gaze. "When you came to us twenty-one years ago, the king and queen took you in and treated you as one of their own. And now that you've come of age—"

"Max?" Eric suddenly realises his dog is no longer beside him. "Max! What are you doing over there? Come here, boy!" His dog is across the ship, panting happily as he tries to peer at the sea over the ship's railing.

The prince bends down to ruffle the fur on his dog's face. "What are you looking at, silly boy?"

* * *

Ariel's heart races as she presses herself into the lifeboat to avoid being seen by the human who has come for 'Max'. Under the sea, they don't have any creatures quite like Max, all big and fluffy with *four* legs! He likes her, if his wagging tail and happy panting are anything to go by.

In the opening, a hand appears, patting Max on the head and guiding him out of her view.

"Eric, now that you've come of age, your responsibilities are at home," someone says. "Your father would have expected that."

"Oh, yes, trapped inside that castle in isolation and fear." Eric's voice is heavy with sarcasm. "I can't do it."

Something in Ariel stirs. Based on his conversation

with the other man, she realises the human's name is Eric and he is a prince. His words are piercing, echoing her own feelings more than anyone has ever been able to. She doesn't know whether to find it comforting or frightening that even in the vast, open human world, someone can feel just as trapped as she does. Maybe it's inevitable for a child of a king.

Ariel may understand, but the human with Eric doesn't seem to. "I believe a little fear may be advisable," he counters.

"Grimsby," Eric groans. "You're not listening. I want to be a different kind of leader. That's the whole reason we're on this voyage. Don't you see? We have to stay open to what's out here. It's the only way our island can grow."

Eric leans over the railing, gazing out to the sea. Ariel shrinks down further, the wood of the lifeboat biting into her back. "I can't explain it, Grims. It's in my blood. Even now I feel there's something out here calling to me."

Ariel allows herself a moment to gaze at his face. She

suddenly realises that this is the first human she's seen up close. How marvellous! *And he's quite beautiful,* she thinks, her face heating slightly. It's the hunger in his expression as he views the open sea. It's the longing in his words. Nothing at all like the barbarians, with sharp teeth and hate in their eyes, that her father described. No, the more Ariel stares, the more she recognises pure wonder in this human's eyes.

Ariel is startled by a few cold drops of water hitting her cheek. She follows Eric's gaze to the darkening clouds on the horizon. His face goes pale.

"Storm coming in fast!" Eric shouts as his crew swarms into motion. Eric moves away from the railing and begins calling out orders. The sky opens up, and a sudden downpour sweeps across the deck. The ship rocks violently back and forth.

Cold dread twists in Ariel's gut at the sight of the storm. It builds to a startling intensity in mere seconds. Torrents of freezing rain make it hard to see clearly. The ship, which seemed so massive moments ago, is pulled almost effortlessly by the churning waves.

There's a sinking feeling in Ariel's chest as she realises that this is how most of the shipwrecks she's explored happen.

Ariel dares a closer look through the railing, watching as Eric takes charge. "Batten down hatches and crates!" he orders. He directs, and people listen. Ariel is fascinated by the way he moves, with purpose and certainty, as if he's led these men through dozens of storms. She wonders if his confidence truly outweighs his fear, or if it's his job as a prince to be that good at pretending.

The ship lurches again, violently rocking Ariel's lifeboat. She dives out to avoid being flipped over. She resurfaces, swimming alongside the vessel as she keeps an eye on the sailors. The storm has to end soon, right? *Please let them get to safety.*

* * *

Eric is terrified. He has never been a fan of storms. They have a history of not boding well for him, and when he was a child, a single clap of thunder used to send him straight to his parents' bedroom. This storm seemed to come without warning, following Grimsby's reprimand so closely Eric half wonders if the universe is trying to berate him, too. But while Grimsby may have a soft spot for him, Eric knows the sea can be unrelenting.

"Clew up and stow the main course – we're over-canvassed!" Eric yells.

"Brail up the foresail!" Mulligan howls against the onslaught of rain.

Crewmen climb the rigging and furl the sail. There is a flash of lightning, and for that moment the world stops. Then at once the wind is back to shrieking as it batters the ship about like it's nothing. A large wave crashes onto the deck, managing to knock the helmsman over. The ship's wheel spins and turns the vessel off course. The ship is now headed straight towards a line of large rocks, and no one is manning the wheel. Eric sprints over to try to steer the ship on course, but it's too late.

Eric is barely able to brace himself as the ship smashes into the rocks. He hits his head against the wheel. There's a sharp pain before everything goes dark.

All around, chaos is unfolding. Men are thrown violently across the deck. A crate breaks loose and crashes against a railing, bursting open to reveal a statue of the prince. The decorative lanterns fall from the mast, catching the sails on fire.

Eric groans, slowly coming to. A strange ringing in his ears blocks out all other sound. A warm light greets him, and for a moment he's reminded of sitting wrapped and cosy with his mother in front of a glowing fireplace. As his vision clears, he realises that the entire deck is on fire. He jumps up, fuelled by the panic coursing through him. "Lifeboats! Abandon ship!"

Crew are jumping overboard into the water as others rush to lower the lifeboats. A cabin boy, no more than twelve, looks over the side of the boat, frozen with fear.

"Into the water, boy!" Mulligan calls.

The boy hesitates, his face pale with panic.

"Argh," Mulligan groans before picking up the boy and throwing him overboard. He jumps in after him.

Grimsby shakily climbs up the rail, his face ghost white as he jumps into the water.

"It's jammed!" Hawkins calls as he unsuccessfully tries to lower a lifeboat.

With no time to lose, Eric grabs Hawkins' machete. "Stand aside!" He cuts through the ropes, sending the lifeboat plummeting into the ocean. The sailors in the water swim to it while the rest continue to abandon ship. Heat from the fire prickles Eric's skin, and he can barely breathe through all the smoke, but he waits until the last of his men have made it over the side. He won't dare leave a sailor behind.

The ship is now completely ablaze. Eric prepares to jump himself when he hears frantic barking. He looks back to see Max is trapped high on the stern castle.

"Max!"

Eric navigates his way through flames. "It's all right, boy," he calls as he reaches the trembling sheepdog. He tosses Max down into the water below. The dog lands with a resounding splash.

His ship is now unrecognisable. All around Eric,

flaming debris falls. He rolls to the side, narrowly avoiding being hit in the head. The ship suddenly lurches, and he is painfully thrown to the opposite side of the deck.

* * *

Ariel has felt fear before, but there's nothing as frightening as her own helplessness as mayhem is unleashed around her. She has seen the aftermath of plenty of shipwrecks, but she has never seen what it's like when they occur. It's terrifying.

She does her best to help, though. As sailors fall into the water and struggle to stay afloat, she pushes drifting lifeboats towards them. She makes sure to stay underwater, out of sight. Luckily, they are too focused on survival to pay close attention, even when she has to give one of the last sailors who jumped a gentle push onto his lifeboat. A nearby splash alerts Ariel to Max, paddling ungracefully. He lets out a low whine when Grimsby calls out to him.

"Max! Come here! You can make it!"

Ariel swims beneath Max, one hand against his belly as she guides him to Grimsby's lifeboat. Max sticks his face down and attempts to lick her cheek before Grimsby grabs a hold of him and pulls him onto the boat. Ariel allows herself a moment of relief. She's glad Max is safe.

Most of the men seem to have made it to the lifeboats, but last Ariel saw, Eric was still on the ship. She surfaces in time to see him thrown across the deck and knocked overboard. Panic swells in her chest as he falls into the water and disappears from sight.

Ariel's heart races as she swims among the wreckage around the boat, searching for Eric. She dives out of the way as the statue of the prince breaks through a railing above her and plummets into the water. Ariel swims deeper, her eyes desperately searching. Then she sees him. He's unconscious, drifting down into the deep. She rushes to him and pulls him into her arms before swimming him up towards the surface.

Chapter
Five

Sitting on a rock jutting out of the ocean, and watching Ariel from a distance, Sebastian wonders if he's getting old. Maybe his eyesight is starting to fail him. There's no other logical explanation, because there is no way that this child is doing what it looks like she's doing. And Sebastian knows that this will end up being *his* fault, and then the king will fillet him and give him to the humans to eat.

He's too young to be eaten!

Sebastian's misery only increases when Scuttle suddenly swoops down and lands on top of him. He swats at her, making a noise of distress. "Get off of me, you fool!"

"Oh, hey!" Scuttle says. She scoots over. "Didn't expect to find you here." She cocks her head as she takes notice of the scene that has been horrifying Sebastian for the last several minutes: Ariel, the *mermaid* princess, lying half on the beach while tending to an unconscious *human* prince. Scuttle blinks in surprise. "I *really* didn't expect to find her here."

"Eh-eh!" Sebastian exclaims as Scuttle hops close for a better look. He does not need this bigmouthed creature making the situation worse. "You listen to me, bird! The king can never hear of this. We are going to forget this ever happened." When Scuttle doesn't respond, Sebastian pulls on her wing, making her squawk. "Are you listening to me?"

Scuttle briefly glances at him before her eyes drift back to Ariel. "Yes."

"This is important, bird. *You* won't tell him, *I* won't tell him, and I will stay in *one* piece. You got it?"

Scuttle nods vigorously. "Got it!" She pauses, her shoulders drooping as she frowns in confusion. "Sorry, what did ya say again?"

Sebastian feels ready to explode into a million little pieces. "I'm a dead crab!"

* * *

The sun was just beginning to stretch over the horizon when Ariel laid Eric on the shore. *Please be okay,* she begs now as she removes seaweed from his face and torso. She gently lifts his head. Relief flows through her when she sees his chest start to rise and fall. His eyes remain closed, but he's alive.

Ariel breathes out slowly, trying to force the residual tendrils of fear away. When she saw Eric sink below the water, limp and unconscious, she didn't think twice before diving down to save him. She knows her father, even her sisters, would see her behaviour as reckless.

But as she looks at Eric, here in front of her and safe, she cannot bring herself to regret it.

It strikes Ariel how small and fragile he appears in this moment. Triton has always made humans out to be large, monstrous, dangerous. Eric, clammy and shivering slightly, couldn't look less dangerous if he tried. Ariel wonders what else her father got wrong about the human world.

She lightly traces a finger along the side of his face, observing him now in the morning light. She wishes they could sit together and talk about all the wonderful places they dream of exploring. She could tell him about how limiting being the sea king's daughter is sometimes. Ariel is aware she doesn't really know him, but after listening to his words on the ship, she feels like she could share all her deepest thoughts and he'd understand. She has never had that before.

Ariel starts to hum as she brushes Eric's hair to the side. She notices a gash on his forehead. He must have been hit when the ship started falling apart. Ariel's cool fingers whisper over the injury. Eric stirs under her touch. He is only partly conscious, but as she starts to sing, her song settles into him.

She would love to stay with him. But when she suddenly hears voices coming from further up the shore, she's reminded that she can't. "Check the cove, men!" someone yells. A group of men and women is approaching from not far off. They must be looking for the prince. Ariel dives into the water before she can be seen.

Just after she leaves, the search party spots Eric and scales down the rocks towards him. Ariel surfaces behind a large rock jutting out of the water and watches them carry Eric away.

"He's alive! Alert the queen!" one of them calls.

Something stirs within Ariel. She knows that this isn't the last she has seen of this world. Maybe fate will someday let her be a part of it.

* * *

Deep in the ocean, Ursula watches Ariel in her large black pearl. The young mermaid hums to herself, distracted and dreamy. Ursula laughs. It's too easy. The mermaid is already in love with the human. She's convinced she has found someone who understands her. Ursula rolls her eyes. Being understood is overrated.

"Wait until Daddy finds out!" Ursula cackles to herself. It will be great. Triton will hit the surface, and that little girl will run straight into Ursula's tentacles. It's all coming along perfectly. Ariel won't even realise that she's the *prawn* in Ursula's game – not until after Ursula rips away Triton's power, which should have been hers all along. With one last glance at Ariel, she slithers off. She has work to do.

* * *

"Ariel, could you give me a hand?"

There's a long awkward beat during which nothing happens. Mala sighs, sharing an annoyed look with her other sisters. It's the umpteenth time today Ariel has completely ignored one of them. She's been absently humming to herself and drawing lazy circles in the current all morning. Ariel has always been more prone to daydreaming than the rest of them, but today she seems to be taking it to a whole new level.

"Ariel!" Mala calls again.

"Oh!" Ariel startles before quickly swimming to Mala. "Sure, of course."

All seven sisters are at Merman's Reef doing their best to clean up the debris from the latest shipwreck. The amount of damage is appalling. The once beautiful reef is covered in a mess of metal, wood, nets and broken glass. Mala feels a rush of anger as she studies several corals that have been practically destroyed.

"Do these humans have any idea how much damage their shipwrecks do?" she demands.

"I don't think they intended to have a shipwreck," Ariel says curtly.

Caspia untangles a piece of rope from the remains of the ship's mast, which has broken off a large section of coral. She shakes her head sombrely at her youngest sister. "They're careless, Ariel. It will take thousands of years for this coral to grow back."

"And they've killed nearly all of the sea fern," Indira adds.

Karina nods in agreement. "They'd kill us, too, if they had the chance."

Ariel shakes her head vehemently. "No! No, they're not *all* like that."

Perla scoffs. "Oh, how would you know? You've never even seen one. You were just a child when Mother died and Father stopped us going to the surface."

"Um…" Ariel clears her throat nervously, realising her mistake. "I just mean *we're* not all the same, so why should humans be?"

She just doesn't understand, Ariel's sisters think. Before any of them can say anything more, a new figure comes into view. The girls all straighten as Triton regards his youngest daughter with a wary expression.

"What about humans?"

Ariel's eyes widen. "What I meant was—"

"Look at what their shipwreck did!" Tamika interrupts.

Triton observes the scene. Fury burns in his chest as

he is reminded what reckless barbarians humans truly are. He shoves his trident roughly into the sand. "They got what they deserved. They are the most dangerous species of all. Spoiling our waters, destroying our reefs, having no respect for the balance of the oceans." He lifts a massive beam off the reef as Ariel's sisters nod in agreement.

Ariel, on the other hand, frowns deeply. "They're not the only ones who have no respect for balance."

Everyone looks at her, but Ariel bites her lip before quickly swimming away.

"Ariel, where are you..." Mala shakes her head and lets out an exasperated sigh. The sisters watch Ariel's retreating form before sharing a look. "What is going on with her?"

Perla waves Mala's concern away. "Oh, she's just at that age when she doesn't want to hang out with her older sisters any more."

"Exactly," Caspia agrees. Her lips quirk up in a grin. "Don't you remember what I was like?"

Mala snorts, and the sisters burst into giggles. They

all remember being teenagers, especially in those moments when first loves completely eradicated their ability to think about anyone or anything else. Ariel must have finally hit that phase.

None of the sisters notice that Triton's interest is piqued as they wonder aloud about whether a lucky merman has finally caught Ariel's eye...

Chapter Six

"I can't believe this," Sebastian grumbles to himself. He's pretty sure he has aged several decades in the past twenty-four hours. When he was a young crab, he used to tell his mother and father of his dream to be a part of the sea king's staff. Such a position would come with honour, prestige... but no. Instead, he's swimming around like a crustacean with his head chopped off, chasing down a silly teenager so that he doesn't *actually* get his head chopped off!

Honestly, how is he supposed to keep watch of her if she won't stay still? Sebastian takes a calming breath. "As long as the king never finds out, everything will be all right," he tells himself. All he needs to do is take Ariel back home. He knows she was around here somewhere…

Sebastian nears the spot where he saw her surface the night before. He sees the entrance to a grotto that's almost perfectly hidden. *Ah, so this must be where that girl's been swimming off to!*

"I just have to be firm with her," he tells himself. He'll make her see that this current fancy is just a passing phase. She will understand that she'll forget all about the human prince in time.

As Sebastian enters the grotto, however, he realises it might take longer than he's been hoping. His jaw drops at the sight of Ariel placing a statue of the human prince at the centre of the grotto.

Yup, I am a dead crab.

"Ariel!"

She spins around towards him, surprise on her face. "Sebastian! How did you find me?"

Wow, this girl is an expert at missing the point. Sebastian looks around in horror. "What is all of this?" Things that do not belong under the sea are stashed in every corner of the space. There is too much for it to all be objects she's collected recently. She has clearly been doing... whatever this is for a while. Sebastian looks back at the garish statue. "What are you doing with that... that thing?"

Instead of looking abashed, Ariel sighs dreamily. "Isn't it beautiful? Look at the longing in his eyes."

"What do you know about longing? What is he doin' *here*?"

"It's from the shipwreck. I found him at Merman's Reef. And I'll bet there's so much more."

Sebastian gapes at her. Why is she talking like fooling around with all these forbidden objects isn't going to get them *both* in trouble? Why doesn't anyone ever think about Sebastian?

Unconcerned by the crab's plight, Ariel swims out of the grotto. Sebastian is dumbfounded. She's just been caught, yet she still thinks this is the time to gather more incriminating evidence.

"No – no! Ariel!" Sebastian hurries after her. "Child, get back here!" He catches up and cuts in front of her. "You have got to let go of this obsession with humans!"

She frowns at him. "I'm not obsessed."

Sebastian snorts. "I may be crusty, but I'm not blind. I saw you the night of the shipwreck."

I've got you now, he thinks as she stops in her tracks.

She turns to him with wide eyes. "What?"

"Your father wants you to stay as far away from them as possible!"

"But why?"

He gives her a pointed look. "You know why."

Ariel huffs and crosses her arms. Sebastian knows exactly the arguments she is remembering. *Humans are cruel. Humans are violent. Humans want to destroy the ocean.* A single trip to the surface won't change that.

But still, she looks at him defiantly. "We don't need

to be afraid of them. I know that now. Sebastian, if you had just seen it up there… the ship rode on the wind and they filled the sky with fire!" She grins, replaying the memory in her mind.

Sebastian shakes his head. The young are always so naive. He can tell she is too enamoured with this seemingly mysterious world to give it up easily. It's time to try a different approach.

"Listen to me. The human world is a mess. Life under the sea is better than anything they got goin' on up there." It is always a mistake to think that things will be better elsewhere. This was something he had been taught as a young crab. Ariel wants to explore the treasures of the human world, but the ocean is teeming with so many incredible things.

All around them the sea comes to life. Humans could never appreciate how magical and musical the world under the waves is. Sebastian draws Ariel's attention to the way the vibrant colours of the clams and turtles and sea plants light up around them. A rhythm builds as the natural music of the sea starts playing. Fish around them seem to dance with exuberance, sharing their own love of their wonderful home.

It makes Sebastian feel alive. It's better under the sea. They don't have to worry about getting *eaten* by humans. Surely Ariel can understand how silly it is to want to be part of a world where all her friends are viewed as food.

The music continues to build as sea creatures all around them join and dance. Humans may think they have the monopoly on good music, but Sebastian knows better. *This* is exactly what he is talking about. And just as Sebastian hoped, the joy is contagious. Ariel soon dances along with them.

Sebastian cheers her on. He thinks she's finally getting it. There's no need to bother with the human world. What do they have? A lot of trouble. But here they have the rhythm of the sea. Sebastian can feel it moving through him. The music carries him, and he knows there is no better place to be than right here. And he has helped Ariel realise—

Sebastian glances up to where Ariel once was and

finds nothing but empty space. A quick glance around confirms that she is gone. The crab sighs.

"Ariel?" he calls, trying to ignore the smidgen of hopelessness creeping its way through him. "Somebody's got to nail that girl's fins to the floor."

Chapter
Seven

Ariel isn't the only one whose silly obsessions are causing some frustration. Above the sea, the morning sun rises over the royal castle, and Queen Selina, the adoptive mother of Prince Eric, sits at the dining table for breakfast. Grimsby sits to her right, but the place set for Eric remains conspicuously untouched.

Grimsby is finishing an update on the crew's recent misadventures. "I'm afraid that most of the cargo is unrecoverable," he says. "A few *minor injuries,* but thanks to Eric's bravery, the men fared well."

Eric's bravery has always been one of his most admirable qualities, but it's also one of the main reasons the queen finds herself in a constant state of worry. Minor injuries, Grimsby says, but there was nothing minor about the panic she felt when her son was brought into the castle half unconscious and bleeding from the head.

He's okay, she reminds herself. She looks up at Grimsby. "Well, thank goodness no lives were lost."

He nods. "Indeed."

The queen sighs. "This restless nature of his concerns me. Undertaking these dangerous voyages—" She cuts off as Eric enters the room. His head is bandaged, and his skin has taken a concerning pallor, but at least he's finally up.

"Any sign of that girl yet, Grimsby?" Eric asks.

Grimsby and the queen exchange glances. After all he's been through, this is the first thing on his mind?

"Have some breakfast, please," the queen insists. She even asked the chef to prepare some of his favourites.

"We looked, sire," Grimsby tells Eric. "There was no girl."

"You were lucky to have made it to shore before you passed out," the queen adds.

Eric shakes his head, with a familiar stubbornness blazing in his eyes. "She was real. She saved my life."

"Sit down, Eric."

"I'm not hungry, Mother."

Why do children never take their own well-being seriously? She couldn't possibly have been this difficult when she was his age.

"I'm worried about you," she says. "You've not been yourself since the shipwreck."

Eric turns to Grimsby. "Have you checked the neighbouring islands?"

"Not all of them, but—"

"Then I will."

At this, Queen Selina must put her foot down. "No, you will not. You are not leaving this castle until you're feeling better." *Especially not to search for some mystery girl no one else has even seen!* she thinks.

Eric pulls the bandage off his head. "I'll feel better when I find her."

His mother crosses her arms. "Do not think you are using this girl as an excuse to run off again, risking your life on some trade ship for the sheer adventure—"

"Sheer adventure?" Eric is incredulous. "I'm reaching out to other cultures, so we don't get left behind. Did you know on this last trip we traded our cane for twenty cases of quinine? They use it in other countries to treat malaria—"

"And where are those twenty cases now? At the bottom of the sea." Eric's intentions are noble, but they aren't enough to lessen the risk of his behaviour. "How many shipwrecks have there been in our waters this year, Prime Minister?"

"Six, Your Majesty."

The queen nods triumphantly. "Did you hear that, Eric?"

Eric holds back a huff of frustration. "Of course I did."

"Shipwrecks, hurricanes – the sea gods are against us! How many times do I have to... They are eroding

our land from under us, stealing it back into the ocean."
Doesn't he see how dangerous it is to be on the waters?
"They would kill us all if they could."

He does scoff then. "That's ridiculous."

"Is it?" his mother asks. "May I remind you that a
deadly shipwreck first brought you to us?" She remembers
that day clearly. It was a miracle that he was found alive,
tiny as he was. He was rushed to the castle, and the
moment she laid eyes on him, she knew he was hers.
Even then she was afraid he wouldn't last the night. But
he was a fighter.

Queen Selina looks at her son. All these years later,
and he's still fighting as hard as ever. "Now I almost
lost you to one the other day," she reminds him, since
he's somehow forgotten. She knows he thinks she's
overreacting, but she can't quiet the tiny voice that tells
her the sea is fighting to take him back. Pulling him into
treacherous waters would probably be the sea gods' cruel
idea of restoring balance. Queen Selina remains resolved.
"We cannot keep tempting fate like this. It has got to
stop."

Eric pauses, frowning. "What does that mean?"

"It means that your responsibilities are here now. So, no more voyages, and no more chasing after girls who don't exist."

"She does exist," he insists, taking a deep breath through his nose. "I just don't know where she is." He storms out of the dining room.

The queen shares a look with Grimsby before sighing. "Well, that went well."

She knows that Eric doesn't like what she's saying, but she will do whatever it takes to get through to him. She has already lost a husband. She's not losing her son to his own foolishness.

* * *

Eric makes his way down the castle path towards the rocky coastline below. The beach is where he ends up whenever he's feeling frustrated or restless. He watches the waves pound against the shore, crashing together like his racing thoughts.

He knows the girl is real. The image may be hazy, but the memory is clear. He remembers the feel of gentle fingers running through his hair. He remembers opening his eyes for a brief moment to see her silhouette. Mostly, he remembers her song. The beautiful melody of her voice has been playing like a loop in his head ever since he was rescued.

For the longest time, all Eric has ever wanted is freedom. He doesn't *hate* being the prince – he loves his kingdom and its people – but most days his chest is filled with an emptiness that he's never been able to perfectly explain to anyone else. Something about the title of prince has always felt unbearably heavy. But when he's out on the sea, there is only the salt in his face and wind in his hair, and the promise of something new. It's usually the only time that empty feeling goes away.

It makes sense that most days Eric's mind was fully occupied by thoughts of seeing the world – for all the reasons he'd told his mother and more. But now? Even he can't say why he is so haunted by thoughts of the mystery girl who saved his life. It's like her song has completely taken him over.

His entire life has felt like a series of unanswered questions. Where is he from? Where is he going? What else is out there for him, for his people? He doesn't want "where is she?" to be another unresolved question. His mother may not understand, but this girl isn't some fantasy he can just get over.

For the first time in ages, Eric feels like something new is beginning. The melody plays again in his head. He closes his eyes and smiles as the waves crash perfectly in time with the song.

Chapter
Eight

Sebastian likes to believe that he is a cool, calm and collected crab. So he definitely hasn't been hiding on the outskirts of the coral palace, panicking after realising that he lost sight of Ariel *again*.

One of the royal guards happens upon him and says, "The sea king requests your presence." Nope, Sebastian is absolutely, positively *fine*.

The guard carries Sebastian into the throne room.

"The crab, Your Majesty." Sebastian is ungracefully dropped at the room's entrance.

"Come over here, Sebastian," King Triton says, beckoning him. The tone of his voice doesn't give any clues as to how he is feeling, but Triton always looks sort of menacing, which does nothing to help Sebastian's nerves. It's that ever-present piercing stare, along with hands that could crush Sebastian into fish food.

"Just breathe, Sebastian," the crab mutters to himself. He moves towards Triton, trying to remind himself to stay calm. *Guilty is as guilty acts.*

"Yes," Sebastian squeaks as he approaches the throne. He clears his throat. "Yes, Your Majesty?" That's better. He doesn't sound nervous at all.

Triton leans in, eyeing Sebastian closely. "Sebastian, have you noticed that Ariel has been acting peculiar lately?"

Oh, no! Sebastian gulps. "Peculiar, sir?"

"Distracted, daydreaming, disappearing for hours… You haven't noticed?"

He knows! Abort mission! "Oh, well, I… um…"

Triton gestures for Sebastian to come closer and taps the arm of his throne.

His little heart beats against his shell as he gets nearer to the king. "I actually haven't, you know… um, that is to say, I didn't…"

"Shhh." Triton's lips pull down in a mock frown as he leans towards Sebastian. "I know you've been keeping something from me."

Sebastian nearly faints. He can't stop his voice from hitching up several octaves. "Keeping something?"

"About Ariel."

"Ariel?"

He knows! He knows, and I'm a dead crab! A chaotic swirl of panicked thoughts races through Sebastian. He can barely register what's happening when Triton puts him into his palm and brings him to eye level.

"Is my little one in love?"

Words shoot out of Sebastian in a rush: "Oh, I tried to stop her, sir! I tried to stop her from going to the surface! I told her to stay away from humans! When I saw her with that statue, I—"

"Humans?" An astonished Triton flings Sebastian. "What about humans?" The sea king rises slowly from his throne, furious lightning crackling in his dark eyes. If possible, the temperature in the throne room drops several degrees.

Uh-oh. Sebastian realises he's made a huge mistake. He looks around, wondering if there's a clam somewhere that can swallow him whole. "Humans? Who said anything about humans?"

* * *

Flounder and Ariel arrive at the grotto. Ariel carries an armful of new treasures from the shipwreck. There were so many things she'd never seen before! She can't wait to ask Scuttle about them.

"Let's just drop these off and go back," she says, setting her bounty down in the centre of the room.

"Don't we have enough already?" Flounder sighs. He's been even more nervous than usual exploring this latest wreck, but nothing can dampen Ariel's excitement.

"Oh, come on, Flounder. We're just getting started—"

"So! You disobeyed me!"

Ariel freezes at her father's booming voice. Terror courses through her as she slowly turns around. Triton, his jaw clenched with rage, appears from behind the prince's statue. Ariel's mouth suddenly feels dry. She has seen her father mad before, but she has never seen the veins burst from his forehead quite like that. His grip on his trident is painfully tight. Flounder squeaks and immediately dives for cover. Sebastian watches uneasily behind the sea king.

"You went to the above world," Triton continues.

"There was a shipwreck," Ariel explains. "A man was drowning. I had to save him." Images of the chaos of that night fly through her mind: the storm batting the sailors' ship around, Eric's limp body sinking below the waves. Nothing could ever make Ariel regret her actions on that night.

Somehow this only makes her father angrier. "You should have let him drown!" he says forcefully, his nostrils flaring. "They're savages."

"You don't know that!" she insists.

"They killed your mother!" His voice breaks slightly, his heavy sadness piercing through his rage.

Ariel shrinks back, and a rush of emotions settles heavily in her chest. "I know that." *Of course* she knows. And she knows how much her father misses her mother. It fuels his anger, but it doesn't make it right. "I know," she repeats. "But *one* man did. Why blame every human? Mother wouldn't."

Triton shakes his head. "That's enough."

He says it with finality, a dismissal of any further discussion. He's not listening to her, not really. He *never* listens, because he thinks she's too young and naive to know how the world is. But she knows what she's saying is true. Ariel reaches towards her father, desperate to make him hear her.

"And Eric had nothing to do with—"

"Eric?" Triton's entire face reddens. "Have you lost your senses completely?"

Ariel shakes her head. She needs her father to understand. "If you had just *heard* him, Father..." She

Ariel is a mermaid who wishes to be on land.

One day Ariel saves Prince Eric from a storm at sea.

Ariel makes a deal with the sea witch to trade her voice to become human. Once on land, she is taken to the prince's castle.

At the castle, the prince argues with his mother as he hopes to find the girl who rescued him from the storm.

Sad that she no longer has a voice, Ariel explores the castle with her new legs.

Ariel finds a room filled with human objects – it reminds her of her grotto!

The room belongs to Prince Eric and is filled with things he has collected.

Eric gives Ariel a jade mermaid.

Eric and Ariel look over maps of the world.

Grimsby, the prime minister, questions if Ariel's arrival has made Eric forget about finding the mystery girl who saved him.

Ariel and Eric travel to the village market.

Ariel and Eric return to the castle late from their day at the market and hide from the queen and Grimsby.

The sea witch disguises herself as Vanessa and plans
to marry the prince.

Ariel breaks the spell and, with her voice returned, Eric
realises she is the one who saved him.

thinks about the heartfelt way he spoke of connecting with other lands, and how he didn't leave his burning ship until every last human and creature had been saved. Her father couldn't possibly find that barbaric. "He's compassionate and kind and—"

"And he's a human. You're a mermaid." Triton gestures unnecessarily to her tail.

"Yes," Ariel says, holding back a frustrated groan. "But that doesn't make us enemies." Why won't he understand?

Triton's eyes are stormy with rage. He's had enough. "Promise me you will never look for him again."

"I can't." Ariel desperately shakes her head. She won't let herself lose that feeling of connection she has found. Just the thought makes her throat tight.

"Promise me, Ariel!" Triton clenches his fists so tightly his knuckles turn white.

"I can't lie to you." Ariel holds back a sob.

As his fury builds, his trident begins to glow. "Promise, Ariel," he says again. "I swear, I will get through to you!" He throws out his arm, pointing his trident at the ledge where Ariel's newest treasures sit. A bolt of energy bursts from the trident, creating an explosion.

"No! Please!" Ariel begs. This is her haven. He can't possibly mean to destroy it!

But her father is lost in his anger. "This ends now!" He swivels, throwing out another blast of energy at Ariel's things. She watches in horror as the wonderful treasures she's collected for so long are blown into thousands of tiny pieces, gone in less than a second. She lets out a sob.

"Father, stop! Please, stop it!"

"It's for your own good," he says simply. Then he takes aim at the prince's statue.

Ariel's heart stops. "Father, *no!*" The statue explodes, crumbling to pieces. Briefly, all sound has disappeared except a dull ringing, almost as if the moment isn't real. But then the sound rushes back, and all Ariel can see are the broken pieces on the ground. The pain in her chest is sharp, heartbreak like she's never felt before. She collapses in front of the rubble.

Anger spent, Triton looks at his daughter. For a moment, he is hit with a pang of remorse. He hates seeing her like this. But he quickly remembers all he has lost and stiffens his resolve.

"Never leave again," he orders, but Ariel does not meet his gaze.

The silence that follows his departure is louder than the yelling. Flounder and Sebastian tentatively approach Ariel. Sebastian reaches out a claw.

"Ariel… I…"

"Just go away," Ariel says, her voice small and broken. She can feel their hesitation, but eventually both Sebastian and Flounder leave. Ariel closes her eyes, wishing this could all just be a bad dream.

Never leave again. Her father's words ring over and over in her head. She feels so small, so *trapped*. She remembers Eric using the same word. *Trapped inside that castle in isolation and fear,* he said. And here she is, held prisoner by her father's fear. But Ariel doesn't want to let fear rule her life. She wants to let her choices be directed by curiosity and unity and openness. In this moment, though, everything seems dark and awful.

Lost in her thoughts, Ariel doesn't notice two new

figures slipping into the grotto. Flotsam and Jetsam circle, creating a vortex through which Ursula's face appears. Her voice echoes throughout the grotto.

"Poor child. Poor, sweet child. He can be so angry. He thinks he knows everything."

"Who are you?" Ariel looks up, frightened. She gazes, mystified, at the watery vision of a strange woman in the vortex.

Ursula places a hand to her chest. "Oh, you must not remember me. I'm Ursula."

Ariel recoils. "The sea witch?"

"The *what*? What has your father told you about me?"

"That you like to stir up trouble between humans and merpeople," Ariel answers.

"Is that what he said?" Ursula purses her lips.

"And that's why he blames you for what happened to my mother." Her father has never told her the full story of what happened to her mother, as talking about her death usually upsets him. He has always made quite clear that Ursula played a big role, though.

"Oh, my dear, that was an accident!" Ursula tuts.

"A sailor's harpoon. I had nothing to do with that. And yet he threw me out of the kingdom. I'm not half the monster he claims I am. And I'm only here to help."

Ariel frowns. Everything she's heard about this woman suggests she isn't trustworthy. "I don't need your help."

Ursula shrugs. "Whatever you say, darling." Her image fades.

"Wait!" Ariel feels something squeeze in her chest at the thought of a missed opportunity. Maybe it's foolish, but right now she feels like she's being crushed by a current and is desperate for a way out. Besides, it can't hurt to hear what she has to say, right?

Ursula's image reappears. "Yes?"

Ariel eyes her with a mix of curiosity and suspicion. "How can you help me?"

The sea witch grins, splitting her face in two. "Come, let's have a real chat, nice and comfortable. My precious ones will show you the way to my home."

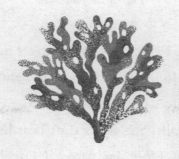

Chapter
Nine

Sebastian and Flounder didn't go far when they left the grotto. They're both still worried about Ariel. Sebastian doesn't think he's ever seen her look so heartbroken. He shifts uncomfortably as a little ball of guilt settles in his stomach.

"She'll be okay, right?" Flounder asks, swimming in nervous circles.

Before Sebastian can answer, a strange sight captures

their attention. Two creepy-looking eels make their way out of the grotto. Ariel follows close behind. Sebastian frowns, discomfort washing over him.

"Ariel?" he calls. She either can't hear him or chooses to ignore him. Flounder gasps beside him. Neither is quite sure what's going on, but it can't be anything good.

"Where is she going with those slippery good-for-nothings?" Sebastian muses. It's still his job to watch over her, so that's what he's going to do. "Let's go," he says, waving Flounder forwards.

* * *

Meeting with Ursula goes against Ariel's better judgement, but there are too many emotions running through her for her to care. Besides, what's the harm in a visit?

Ariel follows Flotsam and Jetsam past the ship graveyard, descending further into the ocean's depths than she typically dares to go. It's much colder than she's used to down here. A chill runs through her as a volcano on one side of her erupts. She isn't sure if she imagines the eels snickering at her obvious discomfort.

They finally start to slow as they reach a giant prehistoric whale skeleton. The sight is gruesome. This can't be where Ursula lives, can it?

But the eels swim straight down into the mouth of the skeleton. Ariel hesitates. She's literally heading towards the belly of the beast. She can almost imagine the creature with a taunting sharp-toothed grin. *Come if you dare,* it seems to say. Ariel briefly shuts her eyes and shakes her nerves away. This is not the time to act like a baby, especially when she chose to come. She follows the eels down.

The inside of the skeleton looks even stranger than the outside. It's covered with ugly serpent-like creatures that seem to be an odd cross between plant and sea animal. They reach out to Ariel as she passes by, grabbing at her arms with cold, slimy tentacles. One wraps itself around her neck. Ariel tries not to panic as she struggles to free herself. With a little force, she manages to rid herself of the creature. She swims a little more quickly after that.

Eventually, they arrive at the entrance of Ursula's lair. Ariel pauses as she takes it in. She shudders when she realises that it's built from skulls and bones of shipwrecked humans. She may be sick.

Ursula, looking quite regal, sits high up in an enormous clamshell. "Come in, come in, child. We mustn't lurk in the passageways." She notices Ariel's distress and pastes on a motherly smile. "Forgive my poor circumstances. I wouldn't choose to live like this, believe me." She gestures at the grim space. "Daddy's been so unfair to both of us – controlling everything we say and do. In a way, we're the same, you and I."

Now there's an unpleasant thought, Ariel muses, trying to keep her expression neutral. She can't think of anyone she'd have less in common with. Then again, what little she does know about Ursula has come from her father.

Ariel looks the sea witch up and down. "You don't seem at all like Father described you." She is not sure how to feel about Ursula yet, but by the way her father talked, she might've expected Ursula to have shark fangs or a cruel gaze that could kill on sight. From what Ariel can tell, she has neither.

Ursula slithers across the obsidian walls of her lair towards Ariel. "Is that right? We never did get along. He always got what he wanted, and what did I get?"

She does not wait for Ariel to answer. "Nothing. *Zip*. *Nada*. Squat." Ursula grins sardonically. "Sound familiar, hon? I know what you're going through, believe me. And I know why you're here."

"I'm not sure I do," Ariel tells her honestly. Following Ursula immediately seemed like a bad idea, but there's something charismatic about her that draws Ariel in. Ariel wants something that will take away the ache in her chest, but she's not sure there's anything that can help. It's not as if Ursula can somehow undo the damage Ariel's father has already done.

Ursula lowers herself, hanging from the ceiling by her tentacles. She's close enough that their noses almost touch. "Oh, please. I've been watching you for a long time now, dearie. What you really want is to be up there in the above world. It's always had your curiosity, and now it's got your heart."

Ariel blinks in surprise. Perhaps she hasn't been as good at hiding her interest in the human world as she thought, but Ursula is hinting at something more. "What do you mean?"

"Oh, you're so young. Don't you see?" Ursula leans in closer, making Ariel shift uncomfortably. "You're meant for each other." Ursula drops from the ceiling and sits at a black mirrored vanity. "I can't bear to see you suffer like this. And as it happens, I can help you."

Meant for each other? Could it be? Ariel is both sceptical and intrigued. "How?"

"The problem is simple. You can't live in that world... *unless* you become a human yourself."

Ariel gasps. "Become human? Is that even possible?"

"My dear, it's what I do. It's what I live for." Ursula grins.

* * *

Ursula can remember being so innocent and full of wonder about magic. That awe is what helped her become the witch she is today. It's a shame that most merfolk these days rarely get to see this kind of power, thanks to Triton. Ariel should consider herself lucky. Ursula feels a thrill. Here is where the real fun begins. It's time to convince Daddy's little princess that she needs Ursula's help.

Reaching out a hand, Ursula gently caresses the side of Ariel's face. "It's like looking into a mirror," she says wistfully. She used to be just as young and impassioned as Ariel, seeking something beyond what the rules of the sea allowed. Oh, how she misses that youthful energy! *But it's time to focus,* Ursula thinks, shaking her head. She launches into her plan. "Here's the deal. I'll whip up a little potion to make you human for three days. Got that? Three days. Before the sun sets on the third day, you and princey must share a kiss – and not just any kiss. The kiss of true love. Too much?"

She grins as the colour drains from Ariel's face. "If you do, you will remain human permanently. But if you don't, you'll turn back into a mermaid, and you belong to me."

As Ariel's shoulders stiffen in alarm, Ursula realises she should soften things a bit. She doesn't want to scare the child off before things get started. Ursula clears her throat and barrels ahead.

"You understand, of course, you'll have to give up your mermaid gifts. You won't have that tail of yours hanging around, dragging you down. You won't be able to breathe underwater – who needs it?" She waves a dismissive hand. "And, of course, you'll have to give up that siren song of yours, because that wouldn't be fair, now would it?" Ursula touches the shell she wears around her neck. "Don't worry. I'll keep it safe and soundless here with me. Have we got a deal?"

For a moment, Ariel appears dumbstruck. Ursula can see the urge in her eyes, though it wrestles against obvious hesitancy. "I... I don't know."

Ursula shrugs. "Well, I just gave you the premium

package, kid." She looks away. "Life's full of tough choices, isn't it?"

Ariel watches her for a beat. Then she shakes her head and starts to leave the lair. "No, this is wrong. I can't do this."

"Fine, then," Ursula calls after her. "Forget about the world above. Go back home to Daddy, and... *never leave again*."

The echo of her father's words stops Ariel in her tracks. Ursula can practically see the thoughts running through her head. The idea of staying in these waters forever, trapped with Triton's rage, is too soul-crushing.

Thanks for your help, Daddy Dearest!

She watches the vulnerability that pours off Ariel in delicious waves. Ursula recognises the exact moment she has the girl. Before Ariel has too much time to think, Ursula points to where most of the potion has already been prepared and instructs Ariel to put one of her scales inside the cauldron.

After ripping a scale from her tail, Ariel watches the blood glistening along its edge. Ursula reaches out a tentacle and snatches it from her. Giddiness flows through Ursula as she drops it inside the cauldron and begins to cast the spell. The cauldron emits a strange mist that swirls around the whole lair. "Now sing!" Ursula calls. "Keep singing!"

The child sings. The sound is music to Ursula's ears. The mist forms into a tentacle-like shape, which floats into Ariel's mouth, reaches down her throat, takes her voice and carries it to the shell around Ursula's neck. The mist intensifies, swirling around Ariel as she slowly starts to transform. It's working! Ariel's tail disappears and is replaced with legs.

Ursula cackles at the sight. "Look at her stupid feet!"

Ariel flails and starts to panic. Her human lungs are beginning to burn. By now she's realising that she won't last long this deep in the sea as a human. She swims desperately through the skeletal ribs at the top of Ursula's lair and heads straight towards the surface. Ursula notices Ariel's crab and fish friend suddenly appear, following at her heels. She rolls her eyes. *Let those imbeciles try to help her.*

Chapter Nine

Flotsam and Jetsam slowly swirl around Ursula, communicating their anxiety through a series of guttural growls. Ursula is not concerned, though. She waves a dismissive tentacle.

"Don't worry, boys." She holds up her nautilus shell and preens at her genius. "She won't stand a chance without her voice." But just in case, Ursula did slip a little something extra into that spell of hers. Ariel will have a hard time making headway, since she won't even remember that she needs to get that kiss. Oh, how Ursula loves a good memory spell! "Now it's just a matter of time. And then she's mine."

The sea witch can't contain her glee, her cackle echoing throughout the seafloor, as her plan beautifully unfolds.

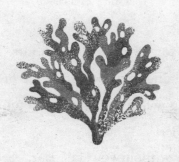

Chapter Ten

Ariel bursts through the surface of the water, gasping for air. She looks around for the shore, but it's barely visible. She struggles as the waves try to pull her under. Sebastian and Flounder surface beside Ariel and help keep her afloat.

"Oh, Ariel…" Sebastian says. He looks between her and the island in the distance. "Well, come on, girl. It's either sink or swim."

They swim for what feels like hours. Flounder and Sebastian are doing their best to guide her, but it's as if they're getting nowhere. Ariel's human muscles feel weak and useless to her.

"Not so easy without your tail, is it?" Sebastian chides her. Ariel wonders if swimming is always this difficult for humans. There's probably a reason humans use ships when they are out this far in the middle of the ocean. Desperately needing to focus on anything else, Ariel shifts her attention to the early-morning sky. Instead of the blue she expects, it's a bright purplish pink, illuminated by rays of sun. The colours remind her of the sea's vibrant corals. It's more proof that these two worlds might not be so different.

If I can just make it there, Ariel thinks tiredly.

"Keep going," Sebastian says encouragingly. "You just got to get your sea legs. We're almost there."

Ariel braces herself, prepared to push her tired limbs just a little further. All at once, the three of them find themselves swept up in a fisherman's net and dropped onto the deck of a small fishing vessel. For a long moment, Ariel feels dazed. She glances up to see a group of seabirds circling her. It looks like Scuttle might be one of them. She then registers the scratchy feeling of the net pressing into her skin and trapping her in the middle of a pile of small fish. It's not very comfortable, but she can't help feeling relief at being out of the water.

It takes a while for the old fisherman on board to notice them, as he's busy swatting seabirds away from his fish. He gasps when he sees Ariel trapped in the net and covered in seaweed.

"Lord have mercy!" He moves to help untangle her. "Are you all right?"

Ariel opens her mouth to say, *I'm okay*. But the words don't come out. No sound comes out. Ariel's eyes widen in surprise as she realises that she can't speak at all.

"You poor girl," the old fisherman tuts. He looks at Ariel with genuine concern. "You must be in shock. I'll go find something to cover you up." He hurries below, muttering to himself, "Another shipwreck. Saints help us!"

In the meantime, Ariel is admiring her new legs with fascination. There are two of them! They are long and brown and smooth. She wiggles her toes and silently giggles at the strange feeling. She has to be the first mermaid who has ever had legs. This feels like a dream.

She tries to rise, eager to stand for the first time. The moment she puts weight on her feet, however, pain shoots through her. She collapses. *How do humans make it look so easy?*

At that moment, Scuttle swoops down onto the boat. She was hoping to steal a fish or two for lunch and is surprised to see a familiar face.

"Say, what's going on, kid? I thought you weren't supposed to be up here. Now you're taking boat rides?"

"That rotten sea witch, she stole your *whole* voice!" Flounder pipes up. He flops out of the pile of fish on deck.

"Oh, hey, Flounder! What are you talking about?" Scuttle asks.

"So, Sebastian told Triton that Ariel saved a human, and Triton got so mad—"

Sebastian climbs out of the pile and interrupts him. "Okay, okay, this is no time to point fins!"

"Hey, hey!" Scuttle says merrily. "Gang's all here!" She loves when her friends are all together.

Sebastian pushes Flounder towards the side of the boat. "Explanations later, man. We got to get you out of here." They don't want him to dry out. Sebastian shoves Flounder overboard through a small opening in the boat's side.

"Wait!" Flounder calls as he falls. "I didn't tell you about the sea witch!" There's a small splash as Flounder hits the water.

"Bye-bye," Sebastian says with a wave. "And don't tell *anyone* about the sea witch."

Scuttle flies to Ariel and cocks her head. "Hmm... something about you seems different." She absently lands on Ariel's feet. "Don't tell me... it's your hairdo, right? 'Cause you've been using the dinglehopper, no?"

Ariel smiles and shakes her head.

Scuttle climbs onto Ariel's knees, peering up at her to try to make sense of it. "I can't – I can't quite figure it out. But I know that if I stand here for long enough—"

"She got legs, you idiot!" Sebastian exclaims, waving his claws in frustration.

Scuttle frowns at him. "You know, we discussed this. I don't like it when you call me an idiot. You know what? It hurts my feelings. Why don't you tell me something nice? Like hey, Scuttle, you know some really cool things. I have some cool things I wanna share with you, too."

Scuttle is interrupted when the old fisherman comes back up from below and swats at her, failing to appreciate the conversation she is trying to have. All he hears is squawking. Humans never seem to understand when animals have something to say.

"Here you are," the old man says, hurrying to cover Ariel with the sailcloth. "It'll have to do for now. I'll take you to the castle. They'll know what to do with you there."

Ariel smiles at this. He's taking her right to see Eric. The old man gives a final nod to assure her that she's all right, then crosses the boat. On his way, he notices Sebastian. He picks up the crab, casually tosses him into a crate along with the other fish, and slams it shut.

The old man introduces himself as they sail. His name is Joshua. He has been a fisherman ever since he was a child. Ariel thinks it must be nice to know exactly where you are supposed to be. She hopes to find that for herself soon. They eventually make it to land, and he helps Ariel into the rear of a cart, where he tucks his crates of fish. He promises she'll be safe and then goes around the front to drive them to the castle. Ariel peers around the side of the cart as it starts to move. She watches the unfamiliar wheel and is amazed by the motion. She brushes her fingers against it and jumps back at the strange feeling.

At this moment it hits Ariel: she's on land! She's overwhelmed with a sense of freedom she has never felt before. She's in a whole new world with endless opportunities to explore. She has *actual legs*.

She makes a second attempt to stand on her own, but the cart hits a bump and she's nearly tossed right out. Ariel never had any idea how much work it is simply to stand. Not that it deters her at all. She knows she'll get there.

For now, a gentle wind dances across her face as they ride along. Ariel beams at the incredible feeling. Wanting to take in everything at once, she finds her head turning every few seconds. She gazes at the surrounding high hills, giant mounds of earth with their tops pressed to the sky. How incredible it would feel to stand at the top and let her fingers graze the clouds! Ahead of them, the castle draws closer. Ariel's heart beats rapidly in anticipation.

Eventually Joshua guides them to the rear gates. He stops at the back entrance and calls out to the servants. "Get Lashana, quick!"

Ariel briefly lets herself wonder who Lashana is, but she's distracted by the enormity of the castle. It's different from her father's underwater palace. It doesn't have the same vibrant colour or the endless movement of the coral reefs, but there's something strong and majestic about this strange building. She can already sense the swift, busy atmosphere as workers immediately begin taking crates of fish from Joshua's cart into the castle. They move effortlessly, like they learnt this choreography long ago.

Joshua carries Ariel through a small kitchen, where a few servants are already washing dishes. Ariel's eyes widen in delight. She watches them dump things into water that is bubblier than any she's ever seen before. There's a rhythm to the way everyone moves in here, just like there was with the people carrying the crates. Ariel tries in vain to see all the unfamiliar trinkets and appliances, but Joshua quickly takes her into a new room.

He sits Ariel, still wrapped in sailcloth, in a chair next to a roaring fireplace. She can't wipe the grin off her face. There are so many things she's never seen before. Her eyes can't decide where to settle.

Lashana, the castle's head of household, hurries into the room. She's simply dressed but holds herself with a clear, kind authority. "Joshua, what is all this?" She takes a surprised step back when she sees Ariel. "What on earth?"

"Girl got tangled in my net," Joshua explains.

"Is she all right?"

Joshua grunts. "She'll survive. She's been through it, though. Won't say a word."

They continue to talk about her, but Ariel doesn't pay them much attention. She's entranced by the fire. The only time she has ever seen fire before was when Eric's ship wrecked. Without the terrifying chaos of the storm getting in the way, she can allow herself to truly admire it. She marvels at the way the yellow-orange flames dance, lighting up the entire chamber. It emits a low, crackling hum with each movement. And the warmth! It's so inviting that Ariel reaches out a hand to touch it, but she flinches back as a flame comes in contact with her finger. *Note to self: touching fire hurts.*

The thought makes her grin. She is in a completely different world, unlike anything she has experienced before. She knows that means making some mistakes. But she ran out of firsts under the sea, and now she has the chance to try things she never thought possible.

Ariel glances down at her new legs. They ache to be

used for the first time, too. Ariel takes a deep breath and tries to stand again. She pushes off her chair and puts her weight on her feet. Unfortunately, she immediately loses her balance and falls over.

Lashana rushes to her side. "Oh, my heavens!" Ariel smiles in thanks as Lashana helps her up, transferring most of Ariel's weight to her. "Let me take you upstairs, get you cleaned up and help you find some clothes."

It's a slow process with Ariel's wobbly legs, and Lashana is practically carrying her, but for Ariel the stairs are another exciting new experience.

Sebastian peers out of one of the fish crates that were brought into the kitchen just in time to see Ariel being led away. He sighs. He's going to need to do his absolute best to keep an eye on this girl.

Chapter Eleven

Upstairs, Lashana leads Ariel into a guest room. She takes Ariel's sailcloth and sits her down in something she calls a bathtub. The tub is cold against Ariel's skin. Lashana didn't explain what Ariel is supposed to do, but Ariel notices the tub looks sort of like a porcelain boat on land. Maybe it needs water?

Suddenly a bucket of steaming water is poured over

her head. Ariel gasps in shock. That wasn't quite what she was thinking. The tub is quickly filled with water far hotter than Ariel is used to. She wonders why humans would subject themselves to this. Lashana then steps away to help Rosa, a young housekeeper, prepare the rest of the room.

"She can't speak at all?" Rosa asks with bewilderment in her voice.

"Can you blame her?" Lashana retorts. "After all she's been through? It's a blessing she's not worse off."

"Such a faraway look in her eyes."

"A bit of soap and a scrub and she'll be good as new."

Ariel doesn't know what soap is, but she isn't sure she'd describe herself as very comfortable in this bath. She continues to scan the room, and she is shocked when her eyes lock onto a dead fish painted on the fireplace tiles. Her mind flashes back to the warnings Sebastian gave her. Ariel's earlier excitement slowly starts to melt into a flutter of nerves. Where does she fit into this strange world?

"I need you to bring me the corset and the other

underthings from the other room. Oh!" Lashana exclaims. "And bring me the blue dress as well."

"Blue dress... I don't remember a blue dress," Rosa muses.

"Child, the blue dress that's in your room."

"No, I'm pretty sure it's green."

"Well, bring me the green dress and then we'll see if it's blue." Lashana sighs.

"Okay... I just thought it was green..."

As Lashana and Rosa continue to talk about gathering clothes, Ariel closes her eyes, steeling herself. She slides down under the water and wills her racing thoughts to settle. The voices around her quiet. This is no time to second-guess her decisions. Life under the sea was lonely, disheartening. She reminds herself of how small it made her feel every time her father refused to listen to her. *As long as you live in my ocean,* he said to her. In Triton's ocean, Ariel was viewed as young and naive. She wasn't allowed to make choices she felt were right. Now, though, she's on land. Things will be different.

Ariel suddenly shoots up, gasping for air. She's never felt such a desperate need for oxygen before. She is hit with the realisation that she can't stay underwater the way she used to. It's not that she didn't know humans can't breathe underwater like mermaids do. Ariel just didn't know it would feel so limiting. Maybe the human world isn't so free. The thought makes her chest tighten.

Lashana, unaware of Ariel's internal struggle, reappears and sticks a strange white bar into Ariel's hands. "There you go. Smells nice, doesn't it?"

Ariel brings it close and takes a big whiff. It *does* smell nice, sweet and a little tangy. This must be what the humans eat. She takes a bite and immediately starts gagging. *That does not taste like it smells!*

Eyes wide, Lashana quickly takes back the bar of soap. "Oh, you poor girl! You must be starving! Rosa, get this child some food – and quick, before she tries to eat the scrub brush."

"Yes, ma'am." Rosa nods and hurries out.

"Right, let's get that seaweed stink off you, girl," Lashana says with a smile.

Ariel is shocked and slightly offended by the comment. She has never minded the smell of seaweed, and she doesn't think she stinks all that bad, either. She does give her arm a quick whiff while Lashana is busy soaping up the brush.

The sensation of being scrubbed is strange but not altogether unpleasant. Ariel likes the white bubbles that now fill the tub. She catches a hint of amusement in Lashana's eyes when she scoops up a handful of suds and blows them back into the water.

Once Ariel is deemed 'perfectly fresh', it's time to get dressed. Ariel discovers that human clothes are confining. Lashana and Rosa squeeze her into boots and a corset laced so tightly that it briefly cuts off Ariel's air supply. She watches in the mirror as layers of clothes are added. It's surreal to see herself dressed this way. It's definitely not what she expected. That's all right, though. It might not be the most comfortable, but apparently this is what many human women choose to wear. And Ariel is giddy to be trying something new. She is also now able to stand on her own. Delighted, she bounces on the balls of her feet.

Lashana and Rosa continue to converse as they struggle to pull a deep blue dress over Ariel's head.

"Those storms are past. They hit us real bad," Lashana says.

Rosa agrees. "Oh, they were nasty. I hope it's the last storm."

"It's hard to believe. Two shipwrecks in one week."

Rosa hums. "Prince Eric's still looking for that girl who saved him."

Ariel pops her head out of the dress, stunned by this news. He's actually looking for her, too?

"Says he won't rest until he's found her."

Lashana and Rosa exchange glances at Ariel's glee, the same thought crossing their minds.

"Stay right here! I'll go get the prince!" Lashana runs out of the room.

Ariel wonders if he will recognise her or if he will feel

the same connection to her that she felt listening to him speak on that boat. What will he say? What will she do? A thousand possibilities run through Ariel's mind, and they all make her smile. She's buzzing with so much energy she can feel it down to her new toes.

* * *

Eric is talking in the main corridor with Grimsby when Lashana rushes towards them.

"Your Highness!" Lashana exclaims. Her expression is both hesitant and excited. "I think... Well, we can't be sure, but I think we may have found her."

Eric immediately knows which *her* she is referring to. A million questions race through his mind as Lashana explains about the shipwrecked girl one of their fishermen brought to the castle this morning. He can figure out the details later, though. Right now, he needs to see her with his own eyes.

He gestures for Lashana to lead the way, and the three of them hurry up the stairs to one of the castle's guest rooms. Eric rushes inside and immediately stops in his tracks.

She's beautiful. It's his first thought. She's in a simple blue dress, and she has warm brown skin and long copper hair past her shoulders. He's sure he's never seen her before, but there's something familiar about her. Wide brown eyes meet his, and they light with a spark. Could it be recognition?

The girl smiles and opens her mouth to say something, then suddenly pauses. Her smile drops, and Eric realises she might be nervous.

"I am so sorry to hear what happened," he says. "What's your name?"

She doesn't answer. She stares back at him, her face pinching into an expression of frustration and helplessness.

"She doesn't speak, sire," Lashana explains.

Eric can't help letting his face fall, feeling the weight in his chest as he realises this girl can't be *the one*. Maybe it was silly to get his hopes up so quickly. He just thought… It doesn't matter. None of the silliness going on in his head is important to this girl. He gives her a friendly smile.

"Well... we're glad you've made it to us. Do you have a place to stay? Family?" The girl lowers her head. Eric senses a deep sadness coming from her. She must have lost more than words would be able to capture anyhow. "Well, then, you're welcome to stay here. For as long as you like." He glances at Lashana. "Make sure she has anything she needs."

Lashana nods. "Yes, Your Highness."

As he turns to leave, Eric catches Grimsby's eye and shakes his head. He glances one last time at the girl as he goes. Grimsby follows him out.

* * *

As Ariel watches Eric leave, she's sure she feels her heart break with his every step. She foolishly expected that getting him to remember her would be easy – that he would look at her and immediately sense some connection. But he didn't even recognise her. Even worse, she caught that brief moment when he wasn't able to hide his disappointment.

Lashana gently places a hand on her shoulder. "We should let you get some rest."

Ariel attempts to smile in gratitude, though she's not sure if she succeeds. Her entire human body feels wobbly. Lashana and Rosa exit, giving her one more sad look before shutting the door and leaving Ariel completely alone – shattered like the treasures her father took from her.

For several moments she just stands and stares at the door, unsure of what to do next. Footsteps echo dully as the women retreat. Slowly, Ariel crosses to the window. She sits on the seat and gazes out at the ocean that was once her home. She marvelled in the feeling of being free from the ocean, but now for the first time she feels truly lost.

A strange sensation on her face surprises her. Ariel puts her fingers to her cheek, and when she pulls them away, they are wet. Tears. Living under the sea, she's never shed them before. They are surprisingly warm, and as they trail down her cheeks and hit the corner of her mouth, she realises they taste like the ocean. Her home. A place that is now painfully far away.

At that thought more tears brim, making Ariel's vision blurry. She instinctively covers her mouth with her hand, though she makes no audible sob. It's an odd experience, crying, but it perfectly captures the hurricane of emotions whirling through her. Like heavy rain in a storm.

Ariel wipes her eyes on her sleeve and stares out the window. She hopes with everything in her that she hasn't made a huge mistake.

Chapter
Twelve

It took longer than Sebastian was comfortable with, but he has finally freed himself from his fish crate prison and is now climbing outside the castle wall onto the window ledge to Ariel's new room. He is exhausted and cranky, and the moment he sees her, it tumbles out.

"This has got to be, without a doubt, the single most humiliating day of my life. Thrown into a crate with a bunch of bottom-feeders. I could have been fricasseed!" He paces in frantic circles. "And then having to climb all the way up here. They couldn't give you a room on the ground floor? Crabs ain't made for climbing! I hope you appreciate what I go through for you, young lady."

She looks away, and Sebastian shakes his head at her. "No. Don't you turn your back on me. What were you thinking, giving up your mermaid gifts?" He pauses to think. There has to be a way out of this. "If we could just get that witch to give them back, you could go home and just be" – he sees the sadness in Ariel's brown eyes and sighs – "just be… just be miserable for the rest of your life. My, what a soft shell I am turning out to be. All right, all right. I'll try to help you. But we've got to be bold, act quickly. Don't forget about the kiss—"

Ariel picks Sebastian up and kisses him.

"Ah, no, not me!" *What a silly child.* "You got to kiss the prince!"

A glazed look comes into Ariel's eyes. Sebastian frowns. "Don't you remember? You've only got three days to…" He stops, realising that she doesn't seem to be hearing his words. Sebastian waves his claw in front of Ariel's face as she stares off to the side. "Hello?"

Ariel doesn't react. Instead, she puts Sebastian down and yawns. Her movements are almost trance-like... Sebastian gasps as it hits him. "Oh, no! She's put a spell on you. You *can't* remember, can you?"

Closing her eyes, Ariel lies down on the window seat. Sebastian is aghast.

"Now what are we going to do?" Of course that nasty sea witch would not play fair. It's not like she wants Ariel to succeed. Well, Sebastian was never a crab to quit. Things just got harder, but not impossible.

"We got no time to lose," he says, filling his voice with optimism. They can definitely do this. "We just got to find a way to get the two of you together, and..." He sees that Ariel is fast asleep. He shakes his head. "You are hopeless, child. You know that? Completely hopeless."

It has been a long day, though. Sebastian decides to follow Ariel's lead and allows himself a brief moment of shut-eye. Unfortunately, he's not even sure his eyes have got to close before he's startled by a ruckus near the window. And sea gods help him, it's that skies-forsaken bird!

Scuttle, having made her way through Ariel's open window, is loudly helping herself to a tray of food left on the nearby table. "Oooo, a buffet! What, no nuts?"

"What are *you* doing here?" Sebastian asks.

"Oh, there you are!" Scuttle pops her head up and beams at him. "I've been looking for you. Flounder told me the whole story. Has Ariel killed the prince yet?"

"Not killed! *Kissed*, you birdbrain! And it's worse than we thought." He sighs, tiredly running a claw over his face. "The witch placed a spell on her. As soon as I tell her she's got to kiss him, the thought jumps clear right out of her head. So now it's up to us."

"To kiss the prince?"

Sebastian groans. Why does he bother? "Forget it."

"Where is Ariel now?" Scuttle asks.

"What do you mean? She's right here—" Sebastian looks behind him and his jaw drops. Ariel's boots lie on the floor, but the girl who should be filling them is gone.

"Oh…" He supposes he shouldn't be surprised. Ariel was never good at staying in one place as a mermaid. Now she's got a brand-new pair of feet to help her evade him.

Sebastian stares longingly at the empty bed. So much for taking a rest. Time to chase after a teenager. Again.

* * *

Ariel sneaks barefoot down the stairs, enjoying the feel of the cool floor against her feet. It's incredible how big the castle is. She wonders how long it would take to explore the entire place. She slips along the hallway, looking into rooms and taking in the myriad unfamiliar sights. Ariel has always known the treasures found in shipwrecks only scratch the surface of what the human world has to offer. She can't believe she's finally seeing it with her own eyes.

The sound of approaching footsteps startles her. She realises she doesn't know if she's meant to be wandering about. She backs into the nearest doorway. Then she peeks to make sure no one saw her. When she sees no one, she sighs in relief and turns around. She's in a three-storey room filled to the brim with objects of different sizes, shapes and colours.

It reminds her a lot of her grotto. The dimly lit space is filled with all manner of treasures collected from around the world – seashells, swords, musical instruments and unusual objects made of jade, silver and gold. The walls are lined with maps and shelves stacked with books.

Overcome with curiosity, Ariel gazes in wonder. She goes around the room, aching to examine everything, not even knowing where to begin. She sees a small figurine that stops her in her tracks. It's a little jade mermaid sitting on a nearby shelf. She turns it around in her hands, admiring it.

At that moment, a frustrated crab skitters into the room.

"What are you doing in here, child?" Sebastian's face is scrunched in exasperation. "You can't just go wandering around wherever you please—"

He's interrupted by the door to the room swinging open. Light streams in from the hall. Ariel and Sebastian both look back in shock, seeing a silhouette in the doorway.

"Hide!" Sebastian whispers urgently. He runs for cover. Ariel moves back into the shadows.

"Who's in here?" someone calls. *Eric.* Ariel would recognise his voice anywhere. He strides past her hiding spot to the window and opens the drapes. Light from the sunset floods through the window, casting the room in a golden-orange glow. Eric draws in a breath when Ariel steps out of the shadows.

"Oh," he says, his shoulders relaxing. "It's you. Nobody usually comes in here." He glances at the mermaid figurine in Ariel's hands. "My little mermaid."

Ariel blinks, surprised, then looks down and realises he's talking about the figurine. She waves her hands to give her best indication that she wasn't trying to take it. She doesn't want him to think she's a thief. She hurries to replace it on the shelf.

"It's all right, it's all right," Eric assures her, a kind smile forming on his lips. "You can look at it. Isn't she beautiful?" He looks lost in a memory as he gazes at the figurine.

Forgetting herself for a moment, Ariel attempts to answer him.

Eric frowns, returning his attention to her. "That's right, you…" He touches his throat in acknowledgement.

Ariel lowers her eyes. Not being able to speak is even more frustrating than she expected.

"Well, it really doesn't matter," Eric continues. "Most people around here use too many words and have nothing to say." He moves to the jade mermaid and takes it from the shelf. "You know, I never believed all that lore about mermaids luring sailors to their deaths."

Ariel brightens at this. He, too, recognises there's more to another world than the falsehoods he's been told. She gazes down at the little statue with a smile on her face. Eric can tell she likes it. He holds it out to her.

"Here, take her."

She couldn't possibly. Ariel shakes her head.

"No, really. I want you to have her." Eric presses it into her hand. It's still warm from his touch. "I'm running out of space as it is." He picks up a brass sphere from the floor and places it on a shelf. "Nearly all these things come from my voyages. I know it must seem silly collecting all this stuff—"

If only Ariel could tell him how not silly it is. She feels right at home in his room of treasures.

Eric notices a sea stone and holds it out to her. "Just look at this fossilised sea stone. Can you believe such amazing things exist down there?"

As she stares at the rock, something tickles the back of Ariel's mind. She takes it from him and suddenly recognises what it is. Without hesitation, she smashes it on the floor.

"No, wait!" Eric cries.

The rock breaks open. Inside is a delicate amber gemstone shining brightly. Ariel reaches down and hands it back to Eric with a grin. She watches him study the gemstone with fascination.

"How did you know that was in there all this time? That's incredible." He then looks up at her, and their eyes meet. In the pit of her stomach is a strange fluttering sensation, unfamiliar but not unpleasant. Both a long time and no time at all seem to pass before Ariel is able to tear her gaze away. She moves to a collection of shells on a table and picks up a conch.

"Oh, that I just picked up from the beach here on the island," Eric says with a shrug.

Within the shell, Sebastian is hiding. Ariel peers inside, and he smiles with a *you got me* grin on his little face. "Hey, girl."

Ariel smirks, quickly plucks Sebastian out, and puts him back among the seashells before Eric can notice. Then Ariel raises the conch to her lips and blows. A long trumpeting note echoes across the room.

"I had no idea you could do that." Eric smiles, astounded.

It's exciting to see him marvel at things from her world. Ariel holds out the shell to him.

"Me?" He hesitates at first, but she urges him to give it a try. "So – okay, really? How do I…"

Ariel leans in, purses her lips tightly, and blows air through them. Eric watches closely. He leans in and imitates her. He manages an impressive blat of sound. He laughs, surprised and delighted. Ariel chuckles silently along with him. This moment feels pretty perfect to her.

* * *

Eric is surprised at how strange it feels to laugh like this. He hasn't done so in a surprisingly long while. This moment feels too good to let go, so he doesn't. He and the girl continue their exploration of the library, his own fascination with his collected treasures growing now that there's someone equally interested to share them with. Sunlight shifts to moonlight as hours pass, and soon he and the girl are huddled together, leaning over a table covered in maps. The girl points excitedly at various land masses, and Eric identifies the different countries and kingdoms. After a little while, she points questioningly to an area on the map that's less marked up than the rest of it.

"Oh, those waters are all uncharted. Wouldn't it be amazing to discover someplace no one's ever seen before?" He looks up, and there's a glint in her eyes that stirs something in him. In that moment he can tell that she understands, and that the adventure of it sounds as magical to her as it always has to him.

The girl opens another map and lays it out upside down. Eric spins it around. An illustration of a familiar castle stares at them.

"Oh, this is our island. We're in that very castle right now." He points to the surrounding village on the map. "Over here's our main village. Our port there was once the busiest in the region… and I'm hoping it will be again one day." He moves to another spot on the map. "And there's a beautiful lagoon with a little waterfall right here, and then all of that is rain forest."

He glances up at her, feeling almost nervous for some reason. "I could show you around if you like."

The girl meets his gaze, her big brown eyes alight with joy.

Eric grins at her, relief flooding through him. "All right. We'll go tomorrow."

Grimsby suddenly appears in the doorway.

"But, sire—"

"Oh, Grimsby – good! We'll need a horse and carriage ready for us in the morning."

"May I have a quiet word, sire?" Grimsby stiffens slightly.

Eric doesn't miss the man's tone, but he chooses to smile good-naturedly. "Of course."

At the door, out of Ariel's earshot, Grimsby speaks quietly to Eric. "We were going to send out all the carriages tomorrow to look for the girl," Grimsby reminds him.

"The girl?" Eric frowns. "Oh – I wasn't thinking." He completely forgot about his mystery girl for the last few hours. "Of course, yes. We must do that, absolutely."

Grimsby gives Eric a look. "And I must remind you, Eric, what your mother said about not leaving the castle until you're feeling much better."

"I feel fine, Grimsby. I feel better than ever." Eric waves him off.

"Yes... I can see that." Grimsby glances from Eric

to the young lady who has so unexpectedly captured the prince's full attention. "I suppose we can spare one carriage, sire."

Eric can hear Grimsby's implications, but this trip is a completely innocent adventure. This girl has obviously been through a lot, and so has Eric. It would do them both good to be out of the castle. His priority is still finding his mystery girl. There is no reason he can't enjoy time with a new friend along the way.

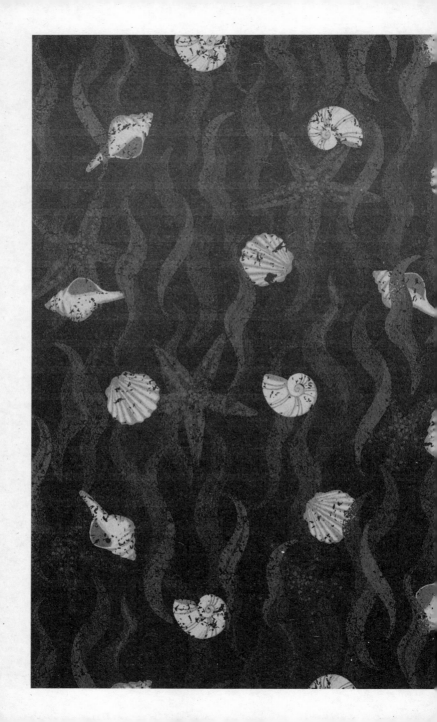

Chapter Thirteen

Triton narrows his eyes at his fidgeting daughters. Perla, Karina and Mala have come with news of Ariel. But it's unusual for the three of them to look this nervous at the same time. He figured that while Ariel was still upset, she would be far more open to interaction with her sisters than with him.

"So," Triton says, gesturing for them to continue, "where is she?"

There's an extended silence as his three daughters shuffle anxiously, their gazes flitting between him, each other and the seafloor. At that moment Triton knows that something is wrong. The throne room seems to darken around them.

Karina frowns. "We don't know, Father."

"She's gone," Perla adds.

Triton stills, an ominous feeling settling around him. "What do you mean she's *gone*?"

The worry on Perla's face does nothing to settle his nerves. "We've been looking for hours. There's no sign of her anywhere. She's not in these waters."

"Then look again!" Triton's hands curl into tight fists. It's all he can do to keep his anger from exploding. *A mermaid cannot just* disappear*! She has to be somewhere.* "Search all the Seven Seas if you have to!"

Karina leans in towards her sisters. "Ariel wouldn't dare go above again, would she?" she whispers, but not so quietly that Triton can't overhear. He stiffens at her words.

"Don't even think such a thing," Perla says, shaking her head. Ariel wouldn't do something that reckless.

"Well, it doesn't make sense," Mala says. "Why would she leave?"

Perla's face falls. "I… I have no idea."

Guilt creeps through Triton as images of his last interaction with Ariel replay in his mind. He hadn't seen her that upset in a long time.

He clears his throat uncomfortably. "Never mind that," he tells his daughters. It's not the time to dwell on the reasons for it. "Just *find her*!"

As his older daughters leave, Triton begins moving restlessly around the room. His guilt is overwhelmed by anger, and if he lets himself peel the layers back enough, maybe he is a little bit afraid.

Triton rubs a hand down his face. He suddenly feels exhausted. What does it say about him that after his years of warnings and overprotection, all his fears still seem to be coming true? The image of Ariel's broken expression flares in his mind again. He knows that he shouldn't have let his anger get the best of him. Maybe this is all his fault. He was already forced to say goodbye to his wife far too early. He can't say goodbye to his little girl, too.

No, he will find her. He will bring her home.

Chapter Fourteen

Eric feels unexpected excitement buzzing through him the next morning. It increases when he makes his way out to the prepared horse and carriage. Grimsby is helping the girl into the carriage. She hasn't noticed Eric yet, but she's already beaming with enthusiasm. He feels his own lips curve upwards. She has a contagious smile. It lights up her entire face. Eric can tell she's eager to see his kingdom.

It has been a while since Eric has explored his own home, but this excursion is the perfect reminder that every now and then the familiar can be fun to look at with a new perspective.

There's a happy bark as Max charges down the stairs and rushes to the carriage. He bounds up onto a box to say hello to the girl inside the carriage. She looks thrilled to see him, too, and immediately nestles the dog into a hug. Max licks her face, making her silently laugh.

The interaction leaves Eric with a warm feeling in his chest that he can't name. After a beat, he picks up Max and sets him back on the ground. "All right, all right," he says, giving the pup a pat. He turns to the girl and smiles. "Looks like you've made a friend there." He says goodbye to Max before climbing into the carriage and taking the reins. "Ready?"

* * *

Sebastian peers out from behind the kitchen door and spies Ariel on her way out with the prince. Panic races through him. "Oh, no. You're not going without me. I only got two days left. I'm a crab on a mission!"

He slips outside and sneaks from hiding place to hiding place, making his way towards the carriage. He's almost there when he's spotted by the prince's mangy mutt! Max barks and bounds towards Sebastian.

Sebastian freezes, terrified. "Oh no, no, no, no! Down, beast!"

He sees the carriage taking off and makes a mad dash for it. He narrowly avoids being caught by Max and leaps onto one of the wheels. He orbits a few times before he's flung up onto the back of the carriage. Neither Ariel nor Eric notice him.

"Yah!". He grins to himself. That landing was pretty impressive. "I still got it!"

* * *

Grimsby is closing the rear castle gates when Lashana comes out and stands alongside him. She squints at the retreating carriage.

"Who is that riding out with Prince Eric?" Her eyes widen slightly in recognition. "Is that the girl who washed up the other day?"

Grimsby nods, though his eyes remain straight ahead. "Yes, it is."

The head of household frowns. "Didn't Queen Selina tell Eric to stay in the castle?"

"Yes, she did."

Lashana raises an eyebrow at Grimsby's unbothered expression. "Won't you be getting in trouble for fetching him a carriage?"

The corner of Grimsby's mouth twitches. He gives her a pointed look. "What carriage, Lashana?" With that, he turns on his heel and goes back inside.

Lashana doesn't miss his full grin, though. She smiles brightly. *Oh, this is going to be good!*

* * *

Eric and Ariel ride out to explore the island. Ariel is particularly intrigued by how the carriage moves.

Eric somehow controls it with the strange ropes in his hands.

He notices her watching and smiles. He offers the ropes to her. "Do you want to try? Here—"

The word is barely out before Ariel takes the ropes and gives them a good snap, like she saw him do at the start of their ride. The carriage soars to an incredible speed that makes Ariel's heart race.

"Look out, look out!" Eric yells. Ariel manages to swerve to avoid a few other carts in the road.

"Sorry about that!" Eric calls over his shoulder. A vendor and his donkey give them an uninterested look in response. "That was close," Eric sighs, spinning back around. "*Whoa!* Watch the... turn!" Eric cries as Ariel manoeuvres the carriage just in time to miss a fruit stand on the side of the road. The move sends the carriage bumping over rocky terrain along the cliff's edge. They bounce along, but Ariel keeps control of the carriage. What an incredible thrill. She loves it! She glances at Eric. A slightly dazed but impressed expression is on his face.

Ariel sees a herd of goats blocking the road ahead. She pulls the carriage to a screeching halt. She and Eric slightly jerk forwards at the sudden stop. Ariel's body buzzes with the adrenaline coursing through her. *What a rush!* Who would have guessed she'd ever get the chance to do something as exciting as *driving*? She relaxes as the world settles around her. The horned, floppy-eared creatures bleat nonchalantly as they stand in the middle of the road. They don't seem interested in moving anytime soon. Ariel looks to Eric, who is catching his breath. He runs a hand through his hair before glancing at her with a light chuckle.

"Well… that was fun…" Eric unsteadily climbs out of the carriage and walks over to help the goat herder move the goats out of the way.

As he busies himself with that, Ariel notices the bright and loud village market nearby. It looks even busier than the castle. This is exactly the kind of place she's been looking forward to seeing. Her feet carry her there with surprising speed. She doesn't want to miss a moment.

People of every shade wearing every manner of colour fill the streets with lively chatter. Ariel marvels at the brightly coloured booths, the delectable smells, the endless swirl of movement around her. She doesn't know where to let her eyes settle.

To her right a man hacks open some sort of hairy brown item with a large knife. He sees her and holds it out. "Fresh coconut!"

Ariel blinks in surprise. *Scuttle was right! They do hate coconut!* She changes course to avoid the coconut killer. Further on, she watches a man grab a fish out of a barrel of water, somehow oblivious to the poor creature's suffering as it squirms about. When the fishmonger's back is to her, Ariel slips past him and pushes the fish back into the water.

She continues to look around in wonder. One man gestures to his jewellery-filled stall – "For the pretty lady?" – while a woman holds out a bowl of something that smells exquisite – "Young lady, would you like to try some?"

Taking the bowl with a wide grin, Ariel turns to leave.

The food vendor calls after her, "Uh, wait – I think you'll be needing this." She hands her a *dinglehopper!*

Ariel knows what this is for! She sets down the bowl, wraps her hair around the dinglehopper and begins to twirl it. She falters when she notices the food vendor gaping at her. She sees several nearby villagers staring at her with confused expressions. She's not sure what she did, but it's clear that she has somehow made a misstep. Ariel's cheeks heat with embarrassment as she gently puts the dinglehopper down and quickly disappears into the crowd.

* * *

Eric has lost the girl already. He has a flutter of worry, since he feels a responsibility to keep her safe, but mostly he is amused. He's not too surprised that a vibrant market like this would pique her curiosity. He can already tell that she's the kind of person who likes getting lost in a new place, exploring everything it has to offer.

He eventually discovers the girl in the midst of a sea

of hats. Grinning, he watches as a vendor holds out one made of straw to her.

"Hat for the lady?"

Eric moves beside her. "There you are."

Her eyes twinkle as they land on him. She smiles as she takes the hat from the vendor and plops it onto his head.

"No, no!" the vendor says, taking the hat from Eric's head. "Try this instead." The man bends to pick out another option for Eric, but as he does, the girl innocently takes the vendor's own hat and places it on Eric's head. The vendor looks up and nods approvingly. Eric chuckles and quickly pays, but by the time he turns back around, the girl has already hurried onwards.

Eric finds her again at a flower stall. He hangs back, taking a moment to watch her survey all the different blossoms with unbridled delight. He doesn't think he's ever seen anyone so thrilled by the simplest of things. It's refreshing. The vendor hands her a flower, and Eric is struck by the thought that it would look lovely tucked into her hair. He immediately feels his face flush.

Then he watches the girl casually take a bite out of the flower before she walks off again. *Did she just...?* Eric stands rooted for several long moments, unable to do anything but rapidly blink at the spot where she stood. He can't help chuckling. *This girl is very strange, but in a good way*, he thinks.

He has to jog to catch up with her again. He finds her admiring swaths of colourful fabric when she suddenly stills. He follows her gaze to two women walking nearby, showing off their sandals to each other. Eric takes her hand and guides her to a stall selling sandals. The whole way there he pretends not to be hyperaware of the feeling of her fingers laced with his. The vendor helps her find a pair of sandals she likes, and she bounces with excitement as Eric goes to buy them for her. Goodness, he's never before met a girl whose joy radiates off her in contagious waves.

Eric is just about to open his coin purse when the girl's attention is captured by something else. She grabs his wrist and tugs him forwards. He barely has time to toss a coin back to the sandal vendor.

The girl leads him through the crowd towards the heart of the village, where a local band is playing island folk songs. A large group of villagers dance to the steel drum rhythm. Eric grins at seeing his people so happy and lively.

At first, the girl seems interested only in watching the locals dance. Then, without warning, she drags him towards a group dancing in the middle. Eric's first instinct is to politely decline. He loves music, but he has never been much of a dancer. When Eric was younger, Grimsby sometimes got in a teasing mood and made fun of the awkward way his gangly limbs moved.

But as the girl holds his hands in hers and starts to move to the music, he knows he won't deny her. And honestly, he's having a lot of fun. The girl isn't the most graceful on her feet, but she dances with freedom and energy. He gives her a quick spin. She only stumbles a little, but it's enough that suddenly they are much closer. Energy moves between them as they sway together. Eric decides that this is one of the best days he's had in a long time.

* * *

A crab peeks past a stall to watch Ariel and Eric dancing close together. *Perfect,* Sebastian thinks. He just needs them to lean in for one little kiss... but the moment passes as they both pull back self-consciously. They are still dancing, but now they're keeping an arm's length apart. But that's not going to help them break the sea witch's spell.

Sebastian sighs in exasperation. His least favourite bird lands nearby and scurries around, looking for scraps. She wanders over when she notices Sebastian.

"Say – any kissing yet?" Scuttle asks him.

"No," Sebastian groans. "When it comes to romance, these two are slow as snails." That girl is lucky she has Sebastian looking out for her. He already has a plan forming in his mind. "Eh – go find Flounder. We got to move this along, and quick!"

"Okay, bossy," Scuttle says, flying off as the humans continue dancing below.

Chapter Fifteen

A little while later, Eric and Ariel are back in the carriage – with Eric driving this time. The sky is painted a lovely purplish blue as dusk begins to settle and stars start to appear.

"I love this time of night," Eric says. It's nice when everything is peaceful like this. It's the quiet calm that emerges just before the world becomes dark. Whenever his mind gets too restless – which is often, honestly –

he likes to stand outside and watch as the moon slowly replaces the sun. All the daytime creatures head for bed as the night ones start to come out. It's a moment of new beginnings.

He wonders if the girl is familiar with any of the wildlife native to this island. He points upwards. "Sometimes you'll see the eyes of a screech owl up in the trees—"

A seabird swooping down from above cuts him off and steals his new hat straight from his head. The bird immediately takes off with it.

"Hey! Come back with that!" Eric stops the carriage and notices the girl's inquisitive gaze. "*That* is not a screech owl." He turns his head back towards the menace. "That's a *thief!* Come on!" he yells as he jumps down and races after the bird. The girl follows, and together they make their way through thick underbrush lining the shore of a little tropical lagoon. Eric takes the girl's hand to guide her carefully through the tangled foliage.

"This way, this way. You all right? Watch out." Eric keeps the seabird in sight, his hat still in its talons. The creature looks back, almost as if making sure they're still following it. Eric frowns. "Hey! Give me my hat back!"

The bird swoops low and drops Eric's hat into one of several rowing boats on shore, then flies away as if it hadn't been leading them on an intense chase.

Eric lets out an amused snort. "All right, then." He and the girl run to the boat. Eric climbs in to retrieve the hat and plops it back onto his head. "Didn't want to lose this," he says with a triumphant smile.

Come to think of it, he has found himself smiling quite a bit today. And he's not yet ready for the day to end. He looks down at the rowing boat. He glances back at the girl. They are in one of the most beautiful lagoons the island has to offer, even if it took a flying thief for them to get here. There's a perfectly good rowing boat here. *It would be a shame to waste it,* Eric thinks. From the look in the girl's eyes, he can tell she has the same idea.

* * *

Scuttle watches Ariel and the prince from a distance with Flounder and Sebastian at her side.

"Move your big fat feathers, bird!" Sebastian exclaims. He swats at her wing. "I can't see a thing."

"Well, they're in the boat," Scuttle explains.

Flounder sighs. "But nothing's happening." The two almost-lovebirds keep looking at each other with shy smiles, but both seem hesitant to make the next move.

Sebastian groans, snapping his claws impatiently. "We're running out of time, and no one's puckered up once!"

Lucky for everyone, Scuttle fancies herself a bit of a connoisseur of all things *love*. She knows exactly what this scene needs to get things moving along. "I think it's time for a little vocal romantic stimulation." She flies up to a low branch, clears her throat, and belts out one of her best.

"Womp womp womp womp woooomp!"

"All right, all right." Sebastian rudely cuts her off. "Listen, Ariel cannot know we're helping. If she sees or hears us, she'll shut us down. Nah, man, we got to be sneaky about this." He grins, his own plan coming into place. "We got to work on the prince – using the power of *suggestion*."

Scuttle and Flounder follow Sebastian into the water and swim inconspicuously towards the rowing boat with him. They hide behind a stand of bamboo reeds.

"Now we just got to set the right mood," Sebastian whispers.

"Good." Flounder nods. "Uh, how are we gonna do that?"

"We got to blend in with the sounds of nature so she doesn't hear us." Sebastian reaches towards the bamboo reeds and begins playing them rhythmically with his claws. "Percussion."

Ooh, brilliant idea, Scuttle thinks. Clearly Sebastian knows a little about the language of love, too. This is why they make the perfect team! Scuttle lands on a nearby leaf, which lowers to reveal a dozen chirping crickets. "Strings," she says.

Flounder jumps out of the water near a flock of birds, which rustle the reeds as they fly off. "Winds."

And Sebastian adds the final piece, hopping on board the rowing boat as it passes by the reeds. He sits behind Eric on the stern, hidden from Ariel's view. "Words." Nothing better than a serenade to get someone to fall in love. Eric may not be able to understand Sebastian, but the crab can try to reach his subconscious. Because of course he wants to kiss the girl.

* * *

The cool night settles around them as Eric rows the boat through a maze of hanging vines. Ariel reaches out to touch the oars, intrigued by how the two paddles can control the entire boat.

"You want to try?" Eric asks.

Ariel nods, smiling. She loves how Eric encourages her to do things she has not done before. He's so easily able to tell when she's interested in something. Like now, he guides her towards him and they begin to row the boat together.

It's so beautiful at night, Ariel thinks. She looks at the sky, dotted with more stars than she could ever count. She's never seen them like this before. They're so bright. It's almost like they're smiling down at her.

Eric smiles up at them, too. "What a clear night. You can see Orion."

Ariel cocks her head. *What's Orion?*

As always, Eric seems to understand the words she's not saying. "The sailors use the constellations to navigate," he explains. He drops the oars, stopping their movement, and leans back. He points to the stars to show her, using his finger to draw shapes of different constellations as he names them.

"That one is Orion, the hunter. There's Aries, the ram. That's Cassiopeia..." He pauses, shaking his head.

"It's funny, I still don't know *your* name. Let me see…"
He thinks for a moment, as if the correct name will just
pop into his mind. "Is it Diana?"

Ariel shakes her head.

"Is it Katherine?"

Ariel shakes her head again.

"Hm, no. Definitely not Katherine," Eric muses.

There's no way he's going to get it without a little help.
After a moment, she gets an idea. She points up at the
constellations he was describing earlier.

Eric frowns. "Sky? Uh…"

She pushes his cheek to direct his line of sight, then
does her best to draw the ram constellation.

"Aries?"

All right, good job. She gestures for him to say it again.
He does, and she holds a hand up to his lips before he
can say the *s* at the end of the word.

"Arie—? Ari-e?" She runs a finger down his lips as he
says it again. "Arie—? Ari-el?"

Yes! She bobs her head excitedly.

Eric grins at her. "Ariel. That's a beautiful name. Written in the stars."

They gaze at each other, and for Ariel it feels magnetic, like everything in this moment was set up just for them. The sounds of nature blanket them in a melody, and the longer she looks at Eric, the closer her body moves of its own accord. Is Eric leaning in, too? Her heartbeat quickens, and her eyes start to flutter closed, and—

Splash!

Suddenly, they are in the water. The boat tipped over. *Well, that's one way to ruin a moment.* They are both sopping wet, but it doesn't lessen the smile on Eric's face. "Well, I suppose now you can say you've had a thorough tour of the lagoon."

Ariel covers her mouth as she giggles silently. She and Eric simply grin at each other for several seconds before he tugs her forwards.

"Come on," he says. "Let's get out of here before we freeze to death."

They leave the overturned boat behind and scramble towards the shore. This was an unexpected end to their day, but Ariel thinks it wasn't necessarily a bad one. As she follows Eric back to their carriage to head to the castle, Ariel can't stop glancing at her hand intertwined with his. It's amazing how perfectly it fits. A warm feeling fills her chest. *No,* she thinks, *not a bad day at all.*

Chapter
Sixteen

The crustacean and his sea friends weren't the only ones watching Ariel and Eric. Down below, Ursula seethes. She saw the lagoon ride through her black pearl, and her entire body shakes with fury as she realises how close that little mermaid came to ruining everything. Too close. She strikes the pearl with her tentacle. It flies across the lair and lands with a loud crack.

"I don't get it. I didn't think that little barracuda stood a chance luring him in without her voice. How is that even possible?" With Ursula's amnesia spell in play, it should have been even more difficult for Ariel to get anywhere with the prince. Had Ursula not been thorough enough in her planning?

"Well, we're not going to let it happen again," Ursula promises herself. Fortunately, her eels are quick thinkers. Flotsam and Jetsam capsized the boat before a kiss could happen, but Ursula knows she can't leave anything to chance now. She needs to hurry and end this.

Ursula rushes to her cabinets and frantically searches through her potions. "It's time Ursula took matters into her own tentacles." She shuffles through the potions, scattering them everywhere, and her panic starts to rise. "Where is it?" she barks, as if she can yell it into existence. "It's got to be here somewhere!"

She cannot have made it this far only to fail now! She knows she has the perfect plan to ensure her success, and this is the time she can't find it? "No, no!" She flings open another cabinet. "Nobody ever puts my things back! Where is it?" She tosses more objects aside, but they are all *useless*! It's not there. She cries out in a rage.

"No, no, nooo!"

Just as she's about ready to yank her hair out, the potion she's looking for floats down into her view. She plucks it with her tentacle.

"Oh. There it is. Got it." Her sinister grin returns to her face as she thinks of what's to come. "That prince won't know what hit him." Ursula is done playing nice. She's worked too hard to let some lovestruck teenager get in the way.

"Only one more sunset. Then I'll make Triton *writhe*." She practically dances with glee as she imagines it. It will be the perfect justice for all she's suffered since Triton exiled her. Did he really think he could banish her without any consequences? *Well, the joke is on you!*

Ursula throws the potion into the cauldron. "I'll see him wriggle like a worm on a hook!" She laughs maniacally as the potion begins to bubble and glow bright.

* * *

Back at the castle, Eric and Ariel try to sneak through the darkened hallways without being seen. Still dripping wet, they carry their shoes in their hands as they move towards the staircase leading up to the guest room. Eric grins at Ariel, who wears his hat on her head.

"Everyone's asleep," he whispers. "We should probably be quiet—"

He's interrupted by his mother's voice sounding from down the hall. "… in his room, all day? I haven't seen him once."

Eric sees the queen and Grimsby approaching them. His mother told him – several times, in fact – that he was not allowed to leave the castle. One look at his drenched appearance and she would immediately know he didn't listen to her. Panicked, he pulls Ariel into a darkened nook, out of view. It's probably silly for him to hide from his mother like this. It makes him feel like a child again, attempting to avoid getting caught breaking the rules. He of course wants to avoid the inevitable scolding, but even more, he hates how upset she always looks when she learns he went against her wishes.

So hiding in a darkened corner it is. Eric catches Ariel looking at him with an amused expression, but she plays along. They stand inches apart, holding their breath and smiling as his mother and Grimsby continue talking.

"I imagine he's in his room resting," Grimsby says. Eric thanks the stars that Grimsby is loyal enough to keep covering for him.

"Has he been avoiding me?" the queen asks.

"No, Your Majesty."

"No?" she asks, seeming surprised.

"No."

There's a pause. "No?" Eric hears the disbelief ringing clear in his mother's voice.

Grimsby makes an impatient sound. "No," he insists.

"You seem awfully certain."

"Avoiding you? That doesn't sound like Eric, does it?"

In fact, it probably sounds a lot like him. He has been more frequently unavailable as his mother has increased talk about buckling down and preparing to become king.

The queen harrumphs. "Then where is he? He's not off searching for that fantasy girl, I hope?"

Grimsby and the queen pass their hiding place, and Eric catches a glimpse of the man's expression as he glances down at the wet footprints they've left. *Oops.*

"No, Your Majesty. *That* I can say with certainty."

"Well, thank heavens for small blessings." The queen steps forwards and nearly slips on a puddle. Luckily, Grimsby catches her. "Are we leaking?" she asks as he steadies her.

Grimsby clears his throat. "Perhaps you should get some rest yourself."

The queen nods. "Yes, I suppose I should… Good night, Grimsby."

"Good night, ma'am."

They continue onwards, their voices disappearing down the hallway.

"Sorry about that. I wasn't supposed to leave the castle today – but I'm glad I did," Eric assures Ariel.

"All these rules…" Simply thinking about it, he feels the weight creep back in, and he has a strong urge to confide in Ariel. He's struck by his certainty that she will understand him. "Truth is I wasn't really born to all this, and it's always made me feel a little uneasy—"

"Welcome back, sire." Grimsby appears suddenly, startling both Eric and Ariel.

"Oh, Grimsby." Eric leads Ariel cautiously out of hiding.

"I trust the two of you had a pleasant outing."

Eric grins as memories of dancing and taking an unexpected lagoon swim fill his mind. He never could have guessed the day would be filled with so much laughter and spontaneity. "Yes, we did," he answers, then looks to confirm with Ariel. "Didn't we?" Ariel nods. "Yes, very nice," Eric repeats.

Grimsby nods to Ariel. "You've had a long day, miss. I imagine we should let you get some sleep." He eyes the pooling water around their feet. "And dried off, as well, perhaps."

"Oh." Eric rubs the back of his neck and chuckles

nervously. "We took a rowing boat out on the lagoon, and I'm afraid we ended up in it."

Ariel beams, nodding to both of them before starting up the staircase. She pauses halfway and turns back. She takes off Eric's hat and places it on his head.

His cheeks warm and he smiles at her. "Good night… Ariel."

She ducks her head happily at the sound of her name. Eric loves the way it feels to finally say it. A part of him just wants to say it over and over and over again. *Ariel.*

Ariel gives him one last wave before she heads up to her room.

Eric watches her as she slowly retreats. He nearly forgets Grimsby is beside him until the man starts speaking.

"About the carriages, sire – I'm afraid they didn't find the mystery girl."

For a moment Eric isn't sure what he is talking about. "They didn't – oh." Of course. How could he forget about his mystery girl?

"May I ask, then, should we continue the search?"

Eric notes Grimsby's expression. "Oh, Grimsby, I— uh— I'm… I feel a little…"

"Confused?" The corner of Grimsby's mouth turns up in an amused way. "If you want the advice of an old man, *allow* yourself to be. There's nothing more beguiling or confusing than the heart."

Eric blinks. "So…"

"So don't be held back by what you think *should* be. Think only of what is. Good night, sire." With that, Grimsby heads off, leaving Eric to ponder his parting words.

Instead of heading back to his room, Eric ends up on the beach where his mystery girl saved him. He stares out at the water, wondering if the waves can send some sign of what he's supposed to do. He has always felt the calling of the sea. It has been a part of his story, and something about whoever saved him seemed connected to that story. He looks back at the castle, where Ariel is, and thinks of these last two days with her. She arrived so unexpectedly, but it already feels like he's known her forever. Maybe his story is ready for a new chapter.

Eric comes to a decision, and he hurries towards the castle to find Ariel. He runs up the path, but a strange sound catches his attention. He stops and looks back towards the ocean.

A dense fog has rolled in. A familiar voice drifts from somewhere along the shore. He freezes, recognising the melody that has haunted him these last days. Almost moving of their own accord, his feet take him down to the rocky coastline. He hears the song, haunting, enchanting, but he doesn't see anyone. Is he being tortured by his own mind? He can't tell if the sound is real or in his head. Then the fog clears and he gasps. Seated on the rocks below is a young woman, her features hidden in the darkness.

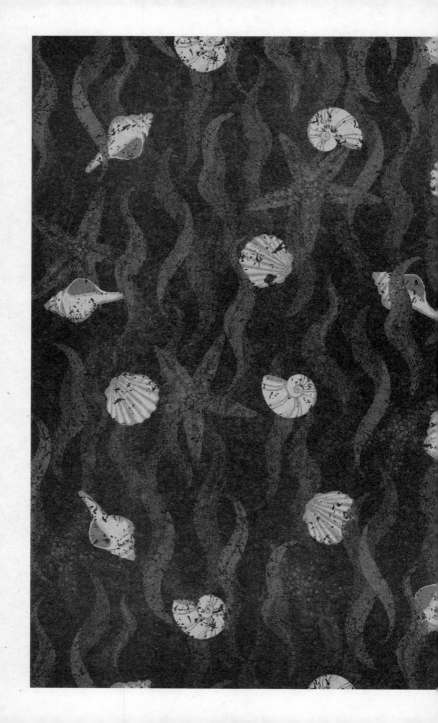

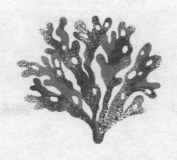

Chapter Seventeen

The next morning, Scuttle flies into Ariel's bedroom. Her feathers are on end from what she overheard during her morning flight around the castle. She shakes her head in exasperation when she finds both Ariel and Sebastian still asleep. *How can they be sleeping when the place is abuzz with such amazing gossip?* The prince is to be married!

Scuttle stirs the two from their sleep and shares

the news. Ariel can barely contain her excitement as she hurries to get ready and races out of the room. Scuttle scooches closer to Sebastian and smiles at him. The crab rolls his eyes.

"Scuttle, you're too close."

* * *

Ariel rushes downstairs to find Eric. Was he really thinking about marriage with her? She knew he had feelings for her, too! She felt flutters when he guided her hands during their boat ride, and warmth whenever they locked eyes, and he seemed to know exactly what she was thinking. Ariel finally knows what it's like to be in love.

As she approaches the dining room, she sees Eric outside on the terrace. She stops when she realises he isn't alone. He's introducing a dark-haired woman Ariel has never seen before to the queen. *Vanessa*, she hears him call her. Ariel ducks behind a pillar to listen.

"I must admit I was mistaken," the queen says to Eric. "My goodness, it is wonderful news, isn't it, Grimsby? It seems you have found the girl of your dreams after all."

Coldness settles in Ariel's chest. *The girl of his dreams?* Wasn't that supposed to be her? She can't remember Eric's ever mentioning another girl to her.

Grimsby hums, though he isn't able to hide the uncertainty in his voice. "Yes, this is quite the surprise, Eric."

"What?" Eric straightens awkwardly. "Oh, I know." There's something off about his tone, but Ariel can't place it. "I know it's fast, but I do owe her my life."

Ariel's brows furrow deeply. *Owes her his life?* But Ariel is the one who saved him from the shipwreck.

"We will celebrate," the queen says. "This evening. You shall introduce your intended to the court. We can make that happen, can't we, Grimsby?"

At least Grimsby looks just as perplexed as Ariel feels. "Yes. If that's what you really want, Eric."

Eric looks slightly distracted. "What I... want?"

That's when it fully hits Ariel. Eric wants someone else. Not her. How could love turn into excruciating heartache so quickly? All she knows is she doesn't want to see any more. Her vision blurs as she runs off, hoping her feet can take her far, far away from here.

* * *

Vanessa can't keep the triumphant smirk off her face, though she tries to tone it down so as not to arouse suspicion. She stands arm in arm with Prince Eric and tightens her grip when he starts to look a little confused.

"It's what we both want," Vanessa assures everyone. And it's true. She may have provided a little assistance to get the prince on board, but things are finally falling into place exactly how Vanessa wants them to.

As they continue discussions, Vanessa clutches the nautilus shell hanging around her neck. No one else notices its gentle glow. They'd never guess that she's keeping Ariel's melodic voice trapped inside it.

* * *

Sebastian is, for the thousandth time in his life, panicking. When Ariel left the room that morning, Sebastian was filled with hope. Now it's late afternoon, and he hasn't seen her for the last several hours. He, Scuttle and Flounder have been scouring everywhere they can think of, but as far as he can tell, the girl has disappeared. Will he never be done chasing this child around?

Worry oozes from Sebastian as he paces on the dock below the castle. "Oh, Ariel, girl, where have you gone?" He perks up as Scuttle lands nearby. "Any sign of her?" *Please say you found her!*

But alas, Scuttle shakes her head. "No luck. I flew over the village three times."

They can't give up. "Check the castle again," Sebastian orders. "We got to find her."

"Copy that!" Scuttle says as she flies off.

Sebastian sighs. "What's wrong with that fool prince, thinking he loves another?" After all the work Sebastian did to get the two of them closer... He knows the prince was falling for Ariel. Sebastian watched him gaze at her with dreamy eyes for an entire lagoon boat ride. There is no way he just decided that he wants to marry another girl. Something is off.

At a distance, Flounder pops his head out of the water. He waves a fin. "Sebastian! Over here!"

The crab scuttles over. "Yes, I'm coming, I'm coming. What is it?"

"I think I know where Ariel is."

"What are we waiting for? Let's go!" Sebastian says as he jumps into the water.

* * *

Ariel sits on the rock where she first watched Eric on the beach. She stares down at her reflection. She thinks the girl looking back at her is so... naive? In truth, she just looks sad. The emotion overwhelms Ariel. She thought journeying to the human world would fill a piece of her that had been missing, but now she's starting to feel like she doesn't belong in either world.

She gave so much to be here with him. Now where is she supposed to go?

Opening her palm, Ariel stares at the little jade mermaid Eric gave her. She watches it slip from her fingers and plop into the sea. Slowly, it sinks down, down, down…

A few moments later, Sebastian climbs onto the rock beside her. "What are you doing, child? You can't give up so easily. That's not like you."

But Ariel shakes her head. Why keep fighting? Humans are not the barbarians her father thinks they are, but maybe Triton was right about one thing. Maybe it is impossible for her ever to really be part of this world.

* * *

Scuttle flies around the castle, still on her own search for Ariel. As she nears the north tower, a familiar voice nearly stops her in her tracks. Scuttle gasps and looks around. "Ariel?"

She lands on the windowsill of the royal guest quarters. There's no Ariel, but something sitting on a table in the middle of the room catches her eye. It's a glowing shell necklace, and it's... singing? It's Ariel's voice; Scuttle is sure of it.

Vanessa emerges from behind a screen. She picks up the necklace and puts it on, and suddenly Ariel's voice is coming from her mouth.

"La da dee, da da da," Vanessa sings. She steps in front of a dressing table and picks up a hairbrush. She throws the brush, shattering a vase. Unbothered, Vanessa spins and falls back onto a chaise.

"So long, Red!"

As Vanessa curls around the chaise to look at herself in the mirror, Scuttle catches a glimpse of the reflection and recoils. To her absolute horror, she sees Ursula, the sea witch!

"Oh, no!" Scuttle gasps. She should have known that nasty witch would be behind all this. She quickly flies off in search of the others. They have to figure out how to take Ursula down once and for all.

Chapter Eighteen

The sun hangs low in the sky, nearly touching the sea at the horizon. Sebastian sits beside Ariel on the rock. Flounder watches sadly from the water below.

"This all has to be some sort of misunderstanding," Sebastian says. "I watched both of you. You're meant to be together." He has never seen Ariel connect so easily with another merperson or sea creature the way she has with Prince Eric over the last few days, and that was without being able to use words! Sebastian knows it wasn't that long ago that he was singing about life under the sea, trying to convince Ariel that there was nothing good for her up in the human world. He will admit that he was wrong. She has truly found something special. He can't allow her to let it go now.

But Ariel just shakes her head. *I won't do it,* her eyes seem to scream. *That girl has always been too stubborn for her own good,* Sebastian thinks.

Before Sebastian can say anything else, Scuttle swoops down beside them. She nearly falls over in exhaustion.

"There you are," she says, half wheezing. "I been lookin' – and I thought I found you, 'cause I *heard*… but then I saw it wasn't *you*, it was *her* – but it *wasn't*… in the mirror. Except she had – she had your *voice*—"

"What are you talking about?" Sebastian yells. Why can't this bird ever just say what she means?

Scuttle gets right up in his face. "Don't you get what I'm telling you?"

"No!"

"The prince has been tricked! That lady who showed up is actually the sea witch in disguise!"

Ariel looks up, her lips parted in shock. Her expression mirrors Sebastian's feelings exactly.

"Are you sure about this?" he asks. He almost doesn't want it to be true, but at least this means Prince Eric didn't fall in love with someone else.

Scuttle squawks in mild offence at any potential doubt. "Of course I'm sure. Have I ever been wrong?" She cocks her head and frowns. "I mean, like, you know, when it counts?"

"Well, what are we gonna do?" Flounder asks, swimming nervously among them.

"Well, we have to do something before Prince Eric ends up with that – that slimy squid!" Sebastian says.

At this, Ariel dives into the ocean and swims towards the castle. *Finally!* Sebastian knew there was some fight left in that girl.

"Yes, girl – go! Flounder, go tell the sea king what's happened. He has to know everything." Triton will probably be mad that Sebastian has hidden this from him for so long, but this is no time to worry about that. If anyone is powerful enough to stop Ursula, it's definitely the sea king. Sebastian has a feeling they will need all the help they can get.

Flounder accepts his mission with a nod. "Okay," he says before he disappears into the water.

"W-what do I do?" Scuttle stammers.

"You give me a lift to the castle. We got to find a way to stall that engagement," Sebastian says. Scuttle gives a determined nod, and Sebastian keeps himself from baulking when she grabs him in her beak. They don't have a single moment to waste. Scuttle carries him off. They've got a wedding to stop.

* * *

The engagement party is well underway. Beautiful harp music floats through the air as people mingle. Grimsby stands with Lashana, and they watch from a distance as Vanessa talks with various members of the court.

"'Heroism' is too strong a word for it," they overhear her saying. "But I suppose I did *save* Eric. After all, it's what anyone would do."

Lashana leans to whisper in Grimsby's ear, "Hard to believe he'd fall for that." Vanessa looks beautiful, of course, but her personality, on the other hand. Well, Lashana is sure she's never met anyone else capable of uttering so many bragging statements in a single breath.

Grimsby hums in agreement. "There's something wrong with this whole business." Eric can be impulsive, but he has been acting different since this woman appeared. Grimsby frowns, eyeing Vanessa with suspicion. There is definitely something off about this woman.

The prince enters the ballroom and heads in Grimsby's direction. Lashana slips away as Eric approaches. A slightly harried expression graces the young prince's face.

"Sire."

"Have you seen Ariel?" Eric asks.

Grimsby clears his throat. "According to the servants, she left the castle early this morning."

The young prince's face falls. "Left?"

"Can you blame her, Eric? I don't understand you. This is not like you." Grimsby would never admit it aloud, but he has been rooting for Ariel and Eric. Lately, Eric has seemed much like a ghost walking the castle halls, until this Ariel showed up. Grimsby could see that she made Eric light up in a way no mystery girl ever could – certainly not someone like Vanessa.

"I'm not really sure I understand it myself. I just wanted to... I thought if I..."

"Eric!" the queen calls from across the room.

"I don't really know what I wanted." Eric shakes his head and sighs.

* * *

Scuttle flies towards the patio, carrying Sebastian in her beak. The sounds of the engagement party drift up towards them.

"Almost there!" Sebastian exclaims. "Now, when I give the signal, you drop me. Got it?"

Of course she does! Scuttle is a master at these sorts of plans.

"Got it!" she replies, opening her mouth to speak.

"No, you idiot!" Sebastian cries as he falls into the water well short of the terrace. Scuttle looks down, confused. Why did he just drop like that? Had Scuttle missed the signal that quickly? Scuttle thinks that was very bad timing on Sebastian's part. He wasn't anywhere near the terrace.

"Guess I'm on my own," Scuttle says, shrugging to herself. Luckily, she's good at improvising. That sea witch won't know what hit her!

* * *

Eric stands beside the queen, watching as she holds out a handkerchief to him. She opens it to reveal a pale blue sapphire ring. The stone in the middle sort of reminds him of the first sea stone he ever collected. This immediately makes him think of Ariel and the stone she smashed on his library floor. Something tugs at his chest. *Don't think about her,* he tells himself. *She's gone now.*

His mother remains oblivious to his uncertainty. She presents the ring with a bright smile. "My darling, this belonged to my mother. I'd like you to have it." She gives him the ring. "Your happiness means everything to me."

The tugging in Eric's chest becomes tighter. *Is this happiness?* he wonders. All his feelings seem strangely muted right now.

They both look up to see Vanessa approaching. The queen kisses her son's cheek before slipping away. "Enjoy yourself."

Vanessa sidles up to Eric. She notices the ring and lets out a gasp. "Oh, Eric! It's beautiful!"

Max bounds towards them. Vanessa cringes back, her expression stuck somewhere between terror and anger. "Get that thing away from me!"

Eric is startled by her reaction. He supposes not everyone likes dogs. He grabs Max by the collar.

"Lashana! Take Max, will you?" The dog tugs against Eric's grip, and he scratches Max's ears to calm him. "Good boy, that's it. C'mon."

Lashana hurries over to look after Max and leads the dog away.

Eric turns back to Vanessa. "Are you all right?"

She gives him a half smile, but it doesn't reach her eyes. "Yes, I'm fine."

At that moment, a seabird dive-bombs Eric. The ring is knocked out of his hand. It bounces across the terrace and disappears under the feet of the guests. Panicked at losing his grandmother's ring after having it for barely five minutes, Eric starts pushing through people to search for it.

"The ring! The ring! I lost— Has anyone seen the ring?"

Grimsby notices the ring has come to rest near his feet. With a quick glance to make sure no one is looking, he gives the ring a kick further into the crowd.

The bird dives again, this time towards Vanessa. Eric is reminded of the bird who stole his hat just yesterday.

It couldn't possibly be the same one, could it? The animal squawks and flaps its wings in Vanessa's face.

"Get off of me, you filthy bird!" Vanessa shrieks. At the same moment, Lashana lets go of Max, who charges at Vanessa. She jumps into the fountain and starts screaming. "Help – I'm being attacked!"

Eric goes to help Vanessa when he suddenly notices someone new entering the room. For a moment, everything else stops. It's Ariel! She came back! He doesn't think twice before running to her.

"Ariel! I've been looking for you all—"

But Ariel pushes past Eric and heads straight for Vanessa.

As Vanessa swats the seabird away, Ariel turns Vanessa around to face her.

"What are you doing?" Vanessa screeches, her face purple with rage.

Ariel grabs at the seashell necklace, pulling Vanessa down as the two of them start to tussle.

"Get her away from me! She's insane!" Vanessa yells.

Behind them, Grimsby is holding Eric back.

The prince struggles uselessly against Grimsby's grip. All around them guests watch the scene with confusion. Finally, Ariel yanks Vanessa's necklace free and sends her tumbling. Ariel stands and slams it to the ground, where it shatters.

A song emerges. Everyone watches it in wonder as a golden mist floats out of the broken shell and up to Ariel's throat, returning her voice to its rightful place. Astonished, Ariel sings out the last note on her own.

Eric stares at her in amazement. "Ariel."

"Yes."

It's the first time he's heard her speak. Yet in hindsight it feels so obvious that it was her all along. "I should have known." He rushes to her. "I don't know what came over me."

"She bewitched you." Ariel spares Vanessa a glance.

"Get away from her!" Vanessa yells. But it's no longer Ariel's beautiful voice she speaks with. It's the bitter, gravelly tone of the sea witch.

Ariel remains focused on Eric. "Eric, I want you to know everything."

Eric shakes his head. "Nothing matters now." He leans in to kiss her. Behind them, the sun is sinking beneath the horizon.

"No!" Vanessa shouts.

Just as their lips are about to touch, the last rays of sunlight disappear.

Chapter Nineteen

Eric is startled as Ariel suddenly gasps and stiffens in pain. Confused, he follows her gaze down as wisps of green mist swirl up around her. *What on earth?* His eyes widen as Ariel's legs fuse together. Ariel immediately begins to sink to the floor, prompting Eric to tighten his hold on her. He slowly looks down again, and where her legs once were is a large shimmery mermaid's tail. With the exception of Vanessa's crazed laughter, it is dead silent.

"Ariel…?" Eric begins, but he isn't sure what to say next. He wants to reassure her. He imagines she's probably frightened right now. Too many emotions are swirling inside him for him to form any proper words, though. Mostly shock, a little bit of confusion. And honestly, there's a tiny thrill blooming, too. The world under the sea – Ariel's world, apparently – has long been of interest to him. Seeing her like this in front of him doesn't seem real.

It is no surprise, unfortunately, that others don't share the sentiment. Behind Eric, his mother staggers back, horrified. "Good Lord! She's a *sea creature!*"

Ariel cowers at the queen's words, tucking her head down in humiliation. Eric feels an urge to wrap her up and hide her away from all the gaping stares.

Vanessa's cackling grows louder. "You're too late!" The queen, Grimsby and all the guests gasp in horror as Vanessa's beautiful human body transforms into the unsettling half-squid form of the sea witch. She throws back her head and laughs manically. "You're too late!"

Releasing her tentacles, she attacks the party guests.

People scream and rush to get out of her radius. The sea witch takes off crawling towards Ariel like a spider, her many tentacles dragging behind her. Without hesitation, Eric scoots in front of Ariel to shield her.

"Stay back!" he calls, sounding much braver than he feels.

The sea witch barely exerts any effort as she knocks him aside with a tentacle.

"Eric!" Ariel yells with panic in her voice.

He barely registers the pain. All he feels is an ice-cold rush of terror as he watches the sea witch dive off the side of the terrace into the ocean below, taking Ariel with her. Eric rushes to the railing, with the queen right behind him. She grips his arm.

"Eric, no! This is the work of the sea gods. I warned you! Their whole world is evil."

He's able to shake free from his mother's grasp. He won't listen to her. He doesn't care if Ariel is a mermaid. They have a connection – one he never knew could be possible for him. There is no way he is going to let some unhinged squid woman hurt her.

"Eric, wait!" his mother calls, but he races down the steps towards the water. He has to get to Ariel. The queen hurries after him, calling out, but Grimsby stops her.

"Let him go, Your Majesty. Let him go."

* * *

Night has begun to fall as Ursula drags Ariel down into the ocean. Ariel fights her all the way, but her physical strength is no match for the sea witch. Flotsam and Jetsam follow close behind them.

"What are you doing?" Ariel asks, still struggling. "Let go of me!"

"Not a chance. You made a deal, remember? Three days, no kiss." A grin full of mockery stretches across Ursula's face. "Is it all starting to come back to you?"

Ariel stops fighting as the memory suddenly hits her. Three days to share true love's kiss. And if she failed? *You belong to me,* Ursula had said. Ariel remembers feeling startled, feeling hesitant when Ursula made her deal inside a swirl of other decorative words and promises.

Ariel *knew* it wasn't a good idea. But her judgement was clouded by hurt and heartbreak. She ignored the tiny voice of reason in the back of her head. She gave Ursula her own scale, effectively signing the deal.

How could I have been so foolish?

Ursula chuckles as she watches realisation creep into Ariel's eyes. "I thought so. Well, now you got to live with it, toots."

In their descent, Ariel's dress catches on a piece of coral and is torn free. She looks back as the dress drifts away, dancing on the tide. She thinks of how close she got to a dream she never expected. She was human. She met someone who stirred up the most wonderful feelings inside her. She was seconds away from their first kiss.

And now she is watching it all slowly float away.

* * *

Triton's blood boils.

When Flounder first came barging into his throne room with a most staggering tale, Triton was immediately overcome with cold dread. Flounder hadn't finished getting his words out before Triton was speeding through the ocean to get to his daughter. He was terrified of what state he would find her in.

As Triton dives past several shipwrecks, Ariel comes into view near a sea ledge. His vision turns red when he sees Ursula's slimy grip on his daughter.

"Ursula!" he bellows. His fury shakes everything around them. Ursula stills as Triton rises from below the ledge, with Flounder beside him. Ursula looks up at him, but she doesn't loosen her grip on his daughter. Triton glares and points his trident at the witch threateningly. "Let her go!"

"Forget it. She belongs to *me* now!" Ursula cries.

Triton seethes. Ursula has already taken so much from him. But while Triton couldn't protect his wife from Ursula, he refuses to allow her to hurt his daughter.

A bolt from his trident ricochets off an energy field shielding both Ursula and Ariel. Flounder rushes for cover.

One of Ursula's tentacles grabs Ariel's tail. She shows

Triton the scar where one of Ariel's scales is missing. "Oh, you see? We made a deal — in *blood!* It's unbreakable, even for you!"

He wants to deny it, to scream at Ursula to cease with such falsehoods. Except the proof is right there in front of him. His daughter is bound, and there's nothing he can do.

Ariel's face crumples as she lets out a choked sob. "I'm sorry, Father. This is all my fault!"

But Triton knows who is truly at fault. He glares at Ursula. "What do you want with my daughter?"

"Oh. Nothing." Ursula grins. "It's *you* I want. I want *you* to suffer the way I've suffered all these years!"

"My wife died because of you!" Raw emotion fills Triton's voice. It's not surprising, but it angers him that even now she doesn't seem the least bit sorry.

"Oh, boo-hoo! You think *that* hurts?" Ursula circles behind Triton and looks over his shoulder at Ariel. "The daughter of the great sea king is a very precious commodity. Poor unfortunate soul—"

Ariel swims upwards in an attempt to escape.

Ursula gestures towards Flotsam and Jetsam. "Get her, boys!"

The eels dart after her and swim in circles around Ariel. Electrical sparks run through their bodies. Triton growls and starts towards her. He'll wring those eels by their necks if they hurt Ariel.

Ursula raises an arm to stop him. "Oh, I wouldn't." They watch Ariel tense as she is enveloped within an electrical vortex. "Shocking, isn't it?"

Aghast, Triton watches as Ariel begins to wilt, the life force draining from her. His entire world stops. He can't be watching his daughter suffering. It feels like his own life is being sucked away.

"Of course, I always was a girl with an eye for a bargain," Ursula continues. She moves towards Ariel. "What do you say to a trade? How much is your precious little Ariel worth to you?"

Triton hasn't always known the right thing to do when it comes to his youngest daughter. They've butted heads countless times. But he does know that he promised himself that he wouldn't see his little girl hurt again. He glances at the trident in his hand. It means nothing compared to the life of his daughter. The sea king sighs in defeat. He lifts the trident and casts it to Ursula, relinquishing his power to save Ariel.

"Hah!" Ursula preens the moment the trident touches her hand. "It's mine now!"

The eels release Ariel. Triton feels a wave of relief as she returns to her former self. It's short-lived, however. The eels grab on to Triton, enveloping him in their electrical vortex.

"No! Oh, no!" Ariel screams.

Ursula laughs uproariously as Triton begins to wilt. He falls backwards off the ledge into the deep. His crown drifts down past Flounder onto the sea shelf.

"Father!" Ariel calls.

Ursula's tentacle picks up the sea king's crown. "At last!" Her cackle rings out loudly, but as she places the crown on her head, the entire ocean goes quiet. It's as if it knows that something terrible has just happened.

* * *

As Ariel watches her father disappear, she feels disorientated, like the entire seafloor has been swept from under her. No one under the sea is supposed to be stronger than Triton. Now he has withered into a husk-like shell, to protect Ariel.

The truth of her father's warnings about Ursula finally sinks in. With her fists curled in fury, Ariel angrily charges at Ursula. "You! You *monster*!"

Ursula effortlessly shoves Ariel aside and aims the glowing trident at her. "Don't be a fool, you little brat! You're powerless against me—"

They are both surprised when she's interrupted by a harpoon flying by her. It nicks her in the shoulder. Ursula cries out in pain. Ariel looks back to see Eric holding his breath in the water. He hovers a few yards above them.

What is he doing here? Though a small part of Ariel is thrilled by the thought of Eric's caring enough to come after her, that part is overwhelmed by the recognition that there is not a more dangerous place for him to be right now. *Get away,* she thinks in his direction.

Ursula glares at Eric, her teeth bared menacingly. "You're going to pay for that!" She sweeps her arm to direct her eels forwards. "After him!"

Eric swims as fast as he can for the surface, with Ursula's slimy eels in close pursuit. He breaks the surface of the water and reaches over the side of his whaling dory for another harpoon. Almost instantly, he's yanked back underwater.

A scream lodges in Ariel's throat as Flotsam and Jetsam latch on to Eric's ankles, pulling him deeper. The trident in Ursula's hands begins to glow as she aims it at him.

"Say goodbye to your human heartthrob!"

"No!" Ariel refuses to let Ursula hurt any more people she cares about. Ariel lunges and pushes the sea witch forwards. The powerful ray from the trident gets redirected, hitting Flotsam and Jetsam instead. The two eels instantly disintegrate. Ariel allows herself a moment of relief as Eric races towards the surface again.

"My babies!" Ursula cries. Despair briefly crosses her face as she stares at the empty space where her minions used to be. Her grief quickly becomes rage.

Ariel races after Eric, knowing Ursula isn't done with them. Giant waves crash violently around them as they surface, even worse than the night Ariel watched Eric's shipwreck. The sky is dark and filled with ominous clouds. It is clear a storm is imminent.

"You have to get to shore," she warns Eric. "She'll kill you." Ariel remembers the fear she felt at seeing him get hurt in the shipwreck just days ago. She didn't really know him at all then. Losing him now? Like this? After all Ariel has already suffered, she doesn't think she'd ever recover.

Eric proves to be just as stubborn as she is, though. "I'm not leaving you," he insists. It both warms and frustrates her.

There's a loud crack of thunder, and the entire sea begins to rumble. Ariel and Eric look down as something bright and sharp breaks the surface of the water between them. Dread forms in Ariel's stomach as she realises that it's Ursula's crown. The sea witch has grown to an enormous size. The waves quake violently as she rises. Ariel and Eric are lifted into the air atop her head. Her maniacal laughter rings out.

"Give me your hand!" Eric tells Ariel. "Now!"

They dive back into the water, now far below them, then resurface. Ursula, wielding her giant glowing trident, towers above them. She truly does look like the kind of monster only nightmares could make up. Her tentacles emerge from the water and splash around her, causing massive waves.

"Look out!" Ariel cries.

One of Ursula's tentacles swings down at them and crashes into the ocean, separating the two of them. Ursula waves the glowing trident above her, creating a violent storm. The dark sky crackles with lightning, casting the world in a chilling glow. Rain pours down in tumultuous sheets. It painfully pelts Ariel's skin. The sea churns, with tall waves rising and attempting to swallow everything in sight.

Ursula towers over it all like a queen of chaos. Her

voice booms like thunder above them. "Now I rule the seas, and all will be helpless under my power!"

Ariel screams as Eric is swept up and thrown by a huge wave. A giant Ursula leans down towards her.

"So much for true love!" the sea witch says mockingly as she lowers the pronged end of the glowing trident into the ocean. She stirs the sea and creates a giant whirlpool. The witch looks on with glee as rotting shipwrecks from below begin to surface, swirling in the whirlpool before her.

Ariel searches frantically among the wreckage and debris. She sees one shipwreck that has a broken mast with a jagged point. Rapidly forming a plan in her head, she swims towards it.

Ursula has her focus on Eric, who has been swept into the current. He's able to grab on to a ship's rigging that has got tangled on a rock, stopping himself from spinning. He looks up at Ursula and blanches as she smiles wickedly at him.

"So long, lover boy!" She aims her trident at Eric and fires a bolt of power through the debris. The bolt blasts away at the rock, but Eric still manages to hold on to the piece of rigging.

Suddenly, the shipwreck with the broken mast rises out of the water with Ariel on the deck. She holds on to the ship for dear life as it rocks forcefully in the storm. Ariel sees Ursula in the distance, and a fierce loathing bubbles in her chest. Ursula caused the death of Ariel's mother. Ursula tricked Ariel and used her to hurt her father. Ursula took a trident that doesn't belong to her and is using its power to cause devastation to Ariel's home. But Ariel will not let the sea witch win. She gathers every ounce of anger and frustration and lets it fuel her with determination. Then she crawls across the deck of the ship.

Raising the trident over Eric, Ursula shatters the last of the rock that his rigging clings to. Ariel's anger flares as she watches him fall. Finally reaching the ship's wheel, Ariel spins it with all the force she can muster. She steers the ship directly towards the sea witch. Ursula's eyes widen in shock as the jagged point of the broken mast pierces her heart. She doubles over, screaming in pain. The impact of the collision throws Ariel to one side of the deck. She pulls herself up on the ship's railing, then looks over just as Ursula's enormous hand reaches out towards her. Ariel dives overboard just in time. Ursula grabs the back of the ship instead, then collapses backwards into the sea, dragging the shipwreck down with her into the depths.

A quiet stillness begins to settle.

Ariel surfaces. Through the slowly dying rain, she's able to see that the violent whirlpool has subsided. Relief fills her chest when she sees that Eric has survived, having got himself to safety on floating debris. She glances down and notices something glistening. The trident has returned to its normal size. It glows as it falls through the water.

Ariel briefly looks back at Eric, torn, before diving after the trident.

Chapter Twenty

The trident falls onto the sea ledge only a moment before Ariel reaches it. There's a tremor, and suddenly the sand swirls up from below. Ariel watches in wonder as her father appears, rising before her, wearing his crown, restored to his former self. She can feel an enormous weight lifting from her shoulders. Her father looks a bit worn and tired, but he's here and he's whole.

Triton's body relaxes as he sees Ariel, as well. He looks

at her with gratitude shining in his eyes. Ariel is the one who should be grateful, though. She doesn't think she has ever been so happy to see her father.

She picks up the trident. "You gave your life for me," she says as she presents it to her father. She has never doubted his love for her, but with the number of disagreements they find themselves in, it is nice to have a powerful reminder that he would do anything for her.

Triton smiles proudly at his daughter as he takes the trident. "And you fought to get my life back."

"I didn't fight alone, Father. Eric was with me—"

He doesn't let her finish. "All that matters now is that you are safe, and home – where you belong."

Ariel deflates, hit with a wave of resignation. Even after everything, her father still clings to his prejudices. She defeated Ursula, yet she feels like she still lost.

* * *

Exhausted, Eric drags himself ashore. As he slowly lifts himself to his feet, he sees that Ariel's dress has washed up further along the beach. Panic seizes him. *What if she's not okay? What if she needs me?*

He suddenly finds himself surrounded by a small crowd – Grimsby, the queen, Lashana and several others from the castle. They make comments of relief at his well-being and try to direct him towards the castle, but Eric pulls away from them. He staggers back into the water. Ariel needs him.

Grimsby hurries after him, reaching for his arm. "Sire, please—"

Eric shakes his head and pulls away again. "We need a boat, Grimsby. We have to find her."

"And then what?" his mother calls.

Her words stop Eric cold. The queen moves up beside him and puts a hand on his shoulder. She doesn't look at him with the tired frustration he'd expect this conversation to bring. Her expression is gentle, sympathetic. Somehow that's almost worse.

"Then what, my love?" she repeats.

Eric shakes his head. What *does* he expect? It's impossible for the two of them to be together now.

They're stuck in separate worlds. Love isn't enough to change that.

"You're right," he says, his shoulders slumping in defeat. "I was chasing a fantasy girl."

"No, Eric." His mother gives his shoulder a comforting squeeze. "I was wrong." Eric wishes he could smile at that. Once upon a time, it would have thrilled him to hear his mother admit to being wrong about anything. All he feels right now is numbness.

His mother continues, her voice soft and earnest. "She was very real. I see that now. And so were your feelings for her. It's just that… this is how it had to end. Our worlds were never meant to be together."

Eric nods after a moment. Despite the ache in his chest, he has to accept the way things must be. He turns away and leads the trek back to the castle.

* * *

Triton likes to think of himself as a good king. He hopes he is, anyway. He has always worked hard to make sure that all merpeople and creatures of the sea are safe and happy. He remembers becoming king, when he was much younger than he is now. He was uncertain of every decision he made. Without his own parents to guide him, how was he supposed to rule the entirety of the Seven Seas?

His late wife always knew how to ground him when the uncertainty became too much. Without her around, he tried hard to prove that he could be the king and the father everyone needed.

Now he sits alone in the throne room, contemplating the last several days. His daughter is back, so everything should be fine. Except Ariel has barely spoken a word since returning to the sea. It doesn't seem to be out of anger or frustration. It's more of a sadness that's palpable when he's around her. Triton feels like there's a heavy sea stone in his chest that he's struggling to understand.

He calls for Sebastian. The crab has been dedicated to keeping an eye on Ariel since all of this started. If anyone can help Triton understand, it's him.

Sebastian makes his way into the throne room. "Yes, Your Majesty?"

Triton stares ahead as he speaks. "I have always tried to do what's best for our people."

"Yes, Your Majesty," Sebastian agrees.

"And what's best for my daughters."

"Indeed, Your Majesty."

"And I've done everything in my power to make *her* happy."

Sebastian hesitates for a few seconds. "Well... not quite."

Triton pauses, waiting for the response he knows is coming.

"I think you need to see to understand, Your Majesty," Sebastian says. And isn't that the crux of it? Triton has always done his best to protect his youngest daughter, but understanding her has always been a little more difficult.

He wants to try, though, so he lets Sebastian lead him to the ocean's surface. For the first time in years, King Triton emerges from the sea. He takes in the blue of the sky, the brightness of the sun, the wispy clouds. It's been a long time since he's had any glimpse of the human world.

Sebastian climbs onto a nearby rock. "Not so bad up here, is it?" he says quietly.

Triton sees Ariel further out, sitting on her own rock and gazing longingly towards shore. She's turned away from them, unaware of their presence. His heart breaks as he watches his daughter. He has always loved how like her mother she is. He especially loves that she shares her smile. He hasn't seen that smile in a long while. It's hard to admit it, but he knows why.

"She wants a different life than I planned for her," Triton says, letting the realisation sink in.

Sebastian hums in agreement. "She did try to tell you, Your Majesty."

That she did. He can't help the waves of anxiety he feels at the mere thought of letting her go. "I won't be able to protect her any more."

"Well, it's like I always say: children got to be free to lead their own lives."

Triton raises an eyebrow at the crab in amusement. "Oh, is that what you always say?"

Sebastian grins sheepishly. "Something like that, yeah."

The sea king looks back at Ariel and sighs. She's so much like her mother, but she is also her own person, and she's stronger than he gives her credit for. He knows what he has to do.

"Well," he says, "there's just one problem left."

"And what's that, Your Majesty?"

"How much I'm going to miss my little one."

Triton lifts his trident and lays it flat on the water's surface. It emits a golden, glittering magic that travels along the water straight towards Ariel. This is his gift to his daughter. He wants her to know that in the end, nothing is more important to him than her happiness.

There's a moment when she turns and their eyes meet. Surprise flickers across her face. He lets himself trust that Ariel will be okay. Her joy is enough for him to know he has made the right decision.

* * *

Eric sits on the steps of the terrace, lost in thought. This pensive mood has been with him for a while. Max bounds up to him with a stick in his mouth, eager to continue the game of fetch Eric has absently been engaging him with.

"Again?" Eric takes the stick and tosses it up the steps onto the terrace. Max goes after it and barks excitedly. It takes Eric a few moments to notice that Max has suddenly gone silent. Eric glances around, but the dog hasn't returned. "Max?"

He glances over his shoulder and his gaze lands on Ariel's smiling face. She stands at the top of the steps, in the same dress from the beach, with Max panting happily beside her.

Eric doesn't waste another moment. He rushes up the steps and takes Ariel into his arms. He relishes the feel of her. She's real. She's here. He leans close and they share a passionate kiss. Eric is met with a sense of rightness. In this moment he is exactly where he is meant to be.

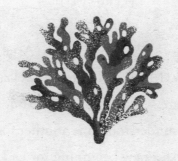

Epilogue

A few weeks later Ariel and Eric run down the rocky path onto the beach as villagers and court members cheer and throw petals into the air. Island musicians play a celebratory tune. Grimsby waits for them down on the sand.

"What's all this, Grims?" Eric asks.

"The queen wanted the two of you to have a proper send-off, sire." Grimsby leads them to Queen Selina, who waits with Lashana and Rosa in attendance.

"Thank you, Your Majesty," Ariel says.

The queen takes Ariel's hand, her fingers brushing

against her mother's ring, which Ariel now wears. "No, thank *you*. Much as I hate farewells, we still have cause to celebrate." She takes Eric's hand, as well. "Our worlds have misunderstood one another for far too long. Your bond marks a new beginning for us."

Ariel likes the sound of that. "Yes, a beginning."

"We learnt a lot from the girl who came to us unable to speak," Grimsby says. Ariel smiles at him warmly.

Eric gathers the queen into a hug. "It's only farewell for now, Mother."

"Oh, I know that." She pulls back. "Now, get out there and change the world – or whatever it is you have to do so we don't get left behind."

"This doesn't sound like my mother." Eric looks to Grimsby with mock alarm. "What have you done with her?"

Everyone laughs. The queen shakes her head before pushing them along with a shooing motion. "Off you go."

The couple starts off down the beach hand in hand.

Lashana calls after them, "Have you decided where you're headed first?"

Eric and Ariel share a look.

"Uncharted waters," Ariel says. With that, the couple hurries off.

With joyous tears in her eyes, Queen Selina watches them go. "It won't be easy for them."

"But they'll have each other," Grimsby says assuredly.

The queen nods. "A mermaid and a man. Whoever would have imagined?"

Who indeed.

* * *

They arrive at the shoreline, where a rowing boat is moored. It will take them to the larger ship in the distance that will carry them to their uncharted waters. As Eric unties the rowing boat, Ariel sees Sebastian, Scuttle and Flounder watching from nearby rocks. She crosses over to them.

"Well, look who's here," she says.

"We got something for you, Ariel," Scuttle says. "Wh-wh-where is it?"

"You're sitting on it, bird." Sebastian pushes Scuttle aside, revealing the jade mermaid Ariel dropped into the ocean.

"My little mermaid!" She starts to reach for it, then pauses. She thinks for a moment. "Actually, keep her for me. Hopefully she causes you less trouble than I did."

"I was right about the dinglehopper, wasn't I?" Scuttle asks.

Ariel laughs but reassures her. "Yes, you were, Scuttle, you were."

"You won't be gone too long, will you, Ariel?" Flounder asks.

"Of course not. I'll be back to see you all by the next Coral Moon."

"Yeah, don't be late this time," Sebastian tells her. Ariel just grins. She'll probably still end up cutting it close.

Eric approaches Ariel as she gazes over the water, a touch of sadness hitting her. "Are you ready?"

She hesitates before nodding. "Yes. Yes, I'm ready."

He helps her climb into the boat. They row out past well-wishers, towards the waiting ship. Ariel looks up in surprise when Eric suddenly stops. She turns and sees her father in the water behind them. Triton gazes upon his youngest daughter, and Ariel sees pride in his eyes. Ariel watches, stunned, as her sisters appear behind Triton – followed by dozens and dozens of merfolk from across the Seven Seas. They've all come to see Ariel off. An incredible warmth spreads through her. Their worlds have united at last.

Triton moves alongside the boat, close to Ariel. "My child…" He looks at the prince beside her. "Eric."

Eric nods in acknowledgement.

Ariel gives her father a grateful smile. "Thank you for hearing me."

"You shouldn't have had to give up your voice to be heard. But now I am listening. And I will always be here for you. We *all* will."

Ariel hugs her father. His embrace is strong and sure. "I love you, Father," she whispers.

He finally lets her go, and with an emotional smile, he pushes the boat, creating a huge wave that sends it gliding gently over the water to the awaiting ship. As everyone around them continues to wave and cheer, Ariel thinks that she has finally found the connection she has always been looking for. It's far better than she ever could have imagined.

Now, she and Eric are off to begin a new adventure. While she has no idea what this journey will bring, Ariel isn't frightened at all. With her family and friends, new and old, behind her, she knows that anything is possible. And what could be more exciting than that?